# KAYAK COMBAT

# KAYAK COMBAT

## Eric Howling

James Lorimer & Company Ltd., Publishers
Toronto

James Lorimer & Company Ltd., Publishers acknowledges the support of the Ontario Arts Council. We acknowledge the support of the Government of Canada through the Canada Book Fund for our publishing activities. We acknowledge the support of the Canada Council for the Arts for our publishing program. We acknowledge the support of the Government of Ontario through the Ontario Media Development Corporation's Ontario Book Initiative.

**Library and Archives Canada Cataloguing in Publication**
Howling, Eric
Kayak combat / Eric Howling.

(Sports stories)
ISBN 978-1-55277-476-2 (pbk)    978-1-55277-477-9 (bound)

I. Title. II. Series: Sports stories (Toronto, Ont.)

PS8615.O9485K39 2010        jC813'.6        C2009-906942-3

James Lorimer & Company Ltd.,
Publishers
317 Adelaide St. West
Suite 1002
Toronto, Ontario
M5V 1P9
www.lorimer.ca

Distributed in the United States by:
Orca Book Publishers
P.O. Box 468
Custer, WA USA
98240-0468

Printed and bound in Canada.

Manufactured by Webcom in Toronto, Ontario, Canada in April 2010.
Job # 367438

# CONTENTS

*For young kayak and canoe paddlers everywhere.*

# 1 COUNTDOWN

The lake was dead calm. Not a wave rippled across the glassy surface. Not a puff of wind blew from the Rocky Mountains. It was an awesome day for a race.

I flipped my hat around and pulled the brim down tight over my hair. My hands clenched the shaft of the paddle. I raised the two black blades in the air, ready to take my first stroke.

I shot a quick glance to the left. Logan was sitting in his kayak, gripping his paddle. Nick was drifting in the lane beyond. They were both staring straight ahead at the bright yellow markers that lined the racecourse. To my right were Nate and Kai in their boats. We were counting down the seconds, listening like hawks for the starting horn to sound. All systems were go.

It was just a training race, but we all wanted to show Coach Wilson who the strongest bantam racer was.

*Brrraaarrr!* The horn from Coach's powerboat blared to start the race. I dug the right end of my paddle hard into the lake. The rounded blade scooped water as I dragged the paddle back along the sides of the kayak. As my right arm pulled, I pushed my left arm forward to start the next stroke on the other side.

*Stroke . . . stroke . . . stroke,* I recited, trying to keep a steady pace. Every stroke was quick, smooth, and powerful. Yellow markers zoomed by, one by one.

I was in lane three and I had to make sure I kept my kayak flying straight. If I crossed into Nate's or Logan's lane, I would be disqualified.

It wasn't long before my arm, shoulder, and stomach muscles started to ache. My heart pounded. I took deep breaths to make sure my lungs were taking in enough oxygen. The finish line was still 500 metres away.

I was working so hard I didn't have time to look around. I wondered where the other racers were. Pulling ahead? Coming up strong from behind? Suddenly, I saw a flash of green to the left. Logan's bow!

Logan was doing his best to pass me. He'd started out slow. But now he looked like he was in high gear. I could see his arms pumping fast. Bursts of white water sprayed after each paddle stroke. If Logan wanted to go head-to-head I was ready. *Bring it,* I thought to myself.

I picked up my stroke rate — from sixty to seventy strokes a minute. I knew I had to keep my count steady to save energy and not burn out before the end. I wondered if I could hold on.

Logan was giving it all he had. His boat shot forward with every stroke. As my kayak knifed through the water I started to speed up and caught him. We were neck and neck. He started to paddle faster and pulled ahead. Nick, Nate, and Kai must have been behind, but I had no idea how far back they were. They could catch up at any second. I dug in and looked down the course.

The large red buoys of the finish line were coming up fast. I just had to hang on a few seconds longer. My shoulders ached. My arms burned. With only a metre to go I drove my blade down through the water for one last powerful stroke, then leaned back so the bow of my kayak lifted up and shot forward across the line. I looked over to see Logan only a stroke behind me. I'd won by a nose.

Logan and I both stopped paddling, totally worn out from the effort. Our bodies slumped forward as we drifted on the lake, still trying to catch our breaths. I don't know if I could have taken one more stroke.

Behind me I could hear Nick, Nate, and Kai fighting for third place. As soon as their kayaks swooshed across the finish line everything went silent. The only sounds I heard were a seagull flying overhead and my friends gasping for air.

I had started paddling back to the dock when I heard a splash. I twisted to my left expecting to see a fish or a bird, but instead I saw Logan's long arms thrashing about in the water. He had dumped.

"You didn't have to fall in just because you lost," I laughed.

"Very funny, dude," Logan said holding on to the side of his flipped kayak.

# 2 PLAYING FAVOURITES

It felt good to win. It had taken me a long time to find a sport I was good at. I'd tried soccer and hockey, but my team was usually on the losing end of the score. Of course, that could have been because of me. I sucked at those sports. And that made me feel like I was always letting my team down. I wanted to play a sport where I had to rely on just myself. If I did well it was because of me. And if I did badly I had no one to blame but me. Two years ago Mom signed me up for a week-long camp at the Alberta Kayak Club. I didn't want to go, but after the first time paddling out on the water I knew I had found my sport. Everything felt right.

Winning let me know that all my hard training was paying off. Even though it was just a practice race, I didn't want any of the other guys to think they could beat Cody Flynn. I hadn't lost a club race yet this summer, and I wasn't about to start now. Logan, Nick, Nate, and Kai were my friends, but when we were out on the water I only saw them as competition.

Coach Wilson sped over to Logan and cut the engine on the powerboat. "Never lose your focus," he scolded, leaning over to help him back into his kayak. "I know you're tired but that's when mistakes are made."

"Sorry, Coach," Logan said, still holding on to his capsized kayak in the water. "Get me back in this rig and I'll catch up with those other floating dudes."

Coach looked at the rest of us. "Time to pack it in, guys," he said. "There's a report of bad weather coming this way. Let's head back." The engine sputtered back to life and churned through the water toward the shore.

I started to paddle across the lake back to the dock. My arms were still rubbery but started to regain strength with every stroke. Even though we didn't have an ounce of energy between us, I still wanted to be the first guy back to the dock.

By the time I reached the long piece of grey plastic jutting out into the lake that served as the kayak launch, Coach Wilson was already standing there. He was wearing the dark sunglasses that he always wore, even when it was cloudy.

Coach had kept a close eye on the race and was busy writing down notes as I paddled up to the side of the dock. "Good job, Cody, but make sure your paddle goes into the water close to the kayak," Coach said, not looking up from his clipboard.

I pulled myself out of the boat and looked to see how far the others were behind me. If you were strong enough and used the right technique, you could flip the kayak up from your waist to your shoulder so it was easier to carry up the paved path to the boathouse. It took a bit of practise, but I had been the first on our team to do it. Most of the other guys had the hang of it now, too. Standing with the long, twelve-kilogram fiberglass boat on my shoulders, I waited halfway up the path to the clubhouse as Logan pulled his kayak up to the dock.

"It's about time," I heard Coach say, frowning down at Logan.

"I was paddling as fast as these muscle-bound arms could go, Coach," Logan joked, making a fist and holding up scrawny arms that seemed too long for a human body.

"Then explain to me how Cody got here five minutes ago," Coach Wilson demanded.

"Beats me, Coach," Logan said, shrugging. "Maybe Cody has a secret motor under his kayak."

"Very funny," Coach Wilson said, but he wasn't laughing.

I turned my face to hide a smile. Logan was a joker, but Coach didn't seem to think he was very funny. Logan never let Coach's criticism get to him, like some of the guys did.

"I think the only secret Cody has is hard work. It's a secret you might want to learn if you ever want to beat him."

"Naw, I don't want to beat Cody. He's my friend. Wouldn't want to make him look bad," Logan joked, whipping his head from side to side to shake the water out of his frizzy red hair.

Coach shook his head at Logan. I remember when he used to shake his head at me like that, too. When I first joined the club a couple of summers ago I thought he was picking on me. It seemed there was always something wrong with the way I was holding the paddle or the way I was sitting in the kayak. Then I realized he wasn't just coming down on me. He was tough on all the new guys. Now that I was winning, Coach was a lot easier on me. Don't get me wrong, he still makes me practise hard, but he doesn't chew me out any more. That honour went to Logan. I liked that Coach thought I was the best.

"Yo, Cody!" Logan yelled, leaving Coach behind and catching up to me. "I almost had you at the finish line."

"Yeah, almost," I said, grinning at him. "Did you see me shoot my boat right at the end?"

"That was an ace move," Logan said.

"Ask Coach to teach it to you," I said. "He showed me."

"Maybe later, dude. I'm not Coach Wilson's favourite paddler right now. Let's stash our boats and get some chow. I'm starving."

Logan fumbled with the kayak, his long, gangly

limbs flying everywhere. No matter how hard he tried, he couldn't quite lift the boat up onto his shoulders. His arms were like giant toothpicks. He just didn't have the muscle. He had to carry the boat at his side with his two hands still wet from his dump in the water.

"Lead the way," I said to Logan.

Logan took a few steps, lugging his kayak up the hill, then twisting around to crack a joke. But just as he turned, the boat slipped from his grasp and crashed to the pavement. Cringing, I looked back toward the dock to see if Coach had been watching, then braced for the hollering that would come if he had been.

# 3 THE MYSTERY PADDLER

I skidded my mountain bike to a stop on the dirt path, the rear wheel sending a cloud of dust and tiny bits of gravel flying into the air. I'd been riding the cliff trail to school when I noticed two ant-sized kayaks skimming across the glassy water of Ghost Lake below.

*Man, I wish I had my binoculars*, I said to myself, shielding the sun from my eyes as I strained to get a better look. I hadn't expected to see anyone out kayaking at this hour. The glacier-fed water would be freezing cold, even on a hot June morning like this.

Maybe it was two adult members of the senior team training before they had to drive to Calgary for work. The club was only a few kilometres north of the city, but living in a small town in the foothills wasn't like the big city at all. There weren't any tall buildings here, just tall trees and lakes carved out of the rolling green forest. Lots of people liked it out here in the country, including my parents. We had a small house, but it was surrounded by a whole acre of land. Mom always

18

said she'd rather have a view of the mountains than of houses packed together in the suburbs.

I readjusted my pack. It was heavy from the books and lunch in my bag, plus the skateboard I had strapped to the back. That morning my mom had made me three PB & J sandwiches for lunch. "Make sure you eat your lunch, Cody," she'd said as I ran out the back door after breakfast. "You need your energy." *Energy, shmenergy.* All I knew was that by the time lunch rolled around I would be triple-cheeseburger-and-fries hungry. Not that I could afford to buy food from the caf every day at school. We weren't rich or anything. Dad was a warden with the Canadian Forestry Service and mom was a waitress at the Blue Water Café overlooking the lake. She had worked there a long time, but now there was talk of a developer buying the restaurant and ripping it down so that a fancy golf course could be built for rich oil executives.

The two paddlers were approaching the dock now, so I decided to check it out to see who they were.

As I pedaled down the slope they came into view. One paddler looked short and strong and wore a white T-shirt — Coach Wilson. I didn't recognize the second paddler, but I could see he was a bit smaller and had blond hair poking out from under a baseball cap.

But finding out who the other paddler was would have to wait if I wanted to get to school early to practise a few tricks with Nick, Nate, and Kai at the skatepark.

Logan wasn't much of a skater and he usually showed up on his bike just before the bell.

The path split in two ahead of me and I took the fork that wound its way through the trees to Evergreen Junior High. I raced along the trail and pulled up in front of the skatepark.

"All right, Cody!" Nick shouted, as he carved a smooth arc around the inside of the giant cement bowl.

Nick's twin, Nate, was right behind him. "Come bank a few turns with us, dude!" he called.

Nick and Nate both had wide-set eyes and long brown hair that streamed out from under their helmets. They were wearing brightly coloured T-shirts and extra-long surfer shorts. The twins may have been average kayakers, but they were awesome skaters.

"What took you so long?" Kai asked, zipping around the bowl like a water bug. Kai had straight black hair and was a bit shorter than me. He was smaller than the rest of us, and lightning fast.

I tightened my helmet and jumped on my deck, sliding into the bowl. We only had a few minutes before school started so we had to make the most of it. I wasn't in the same league as Nick and Nate, but I liked to goofy-foot across the bowl and then reverse for a fakie.

I was holding my own when another skater came screaming across the bowl, did an amazing kickflip, and cut me off.

"Hey, watch it!" I shouted, bailing off my board.

The skater ground to an immediate stop, kicked up his board, and did a 180 turn to face me. The only thing was, he was a *she*.

"Sorry about that," the girl said with a smile. Big brown eyes framed by wisps of blond hair stared down at me. "I haven't skated much lately and I'm just getting back in the groove."

I didn't know what to say. I felt my face turn red. Just then the bell rang, and she took off. Normally I'd be angry if someone cut me off like that, but I'd just been knocked off my board by the cutest skater girl I'd ever seen.

# 4 FRIENDLY COMPETITION

"Hey, Logan," I called, struggling to shove my backpack and skateboard into my locker at the kayaking club. I had a pile of stuff — sandals, sunglasses, sunscreen, granola bars, a Simpsons comic, a towel, water bottle, plus an extra T-shirt and shorts in case I dumped into the icy water. If that happened you had to change your clothes fast. "Did you see who was out kayaking with Coach Wilson this morning?"

"Yeah, I spotted them on my way to school, too," Logan said. "But I've never seen the other dude before. Probably a ringer Coach knows."

After I'd managed to slam my locker shut, Logan and I headed outside to wait for the rest of the Bantam Sprint Team to show. Until summer vacation started in a couple weeks, practices were being held after school. The kayaking season starts when the ice melts on the lake in April and runs until October, when the weather turns cold again.

Out on the water a group of kids were having

kayaking lessons. Some of them were the same age as us, but they didn't qualify for the sprint team. They weren't good enough to race in the regattas.

Looking farther out over the lake, I could see two boats gliding side by side through the water, the paddlers matching each other stroke for stroke. There was a breeze blowing, but their bows cut right through the small waves. They were powering through the water fast — faster than I could go.

I was pretty sure that one of them was Coach Wilson. The other was the mystery paddler I'd seen that morning. *Why is Coach spending so much time with that kayaker?* I wondered.

"What's going down, guys?"

Turning around, I saw Nick flicking his long hair back as he called to us. Nate and Kai were with him.

"Coach and some pro are coming in," I said.

"I think it's some dude he knows from the Canadian team," Logan said.

"Maybe it's Matt Marshall," Nate guessed.

"Matt Marshall!" Kai repeated, his dark eyes growing wide. "That would be awesome."

Everyone had heard of Matt Marshall, the captain of the Canadian Kayaking team. But not everyone knew how Coach almost beat him at the Olympic Trials Regatta a few years ago. The only reason I knew is because I Googled it on the web. I still don't know the whole story because Coach never talks about it. He just clams up when anyone asks him, like it was some big secret.

"Incoming!" Logan shouted.

All five of us ran down to the dock to get a closer look. A few seconds later we stopped dead in our tracks. Coach Wilson and the mystery paddler had pulled up beside the dock and were lifting themselves out of their boats. But the mystery paddler wasn't Matt Marshall or anyone else from the Canadian team. He wasn't even an adult — he was about the same age we were!

Coach Wilson stood up on the dock and surveyed the Bantam Sprint Team. "I have an announcement to make."

Coach patted the new paddler on the shoulder. He scanned from face to face and stopped at me. "I'd like you to meet Tanner Blake," he said, staring me right in the eye. "Tanner is the newest member of our sprint team. He just arrived from Toronto, where he was the best thirteen-year-old paddler at the Maple Leaf Kayak Club. Let's all give him a warm Alberta welcome." Coach beamed.

Waves slapped against the side of the dock. A crow cawed overhead. No one said a word. I stood there with Logan and my other teammates, wondering what just happened. For over a year, the five of us had raced together. We were known throughout the club and on the regatta circuit. Now here was this new guy crashing our team. He was a whole year older than we were and a lot bigger.

Logan broke the silence. "Welcome to the club," he

said, stretching out a long arm for a handshake. "You totally rocked out there."

Tanner crossed his bulging arms over his chest. "I'm looking forward to beating you all . . . I mean . . . meeting you all." Then he laughed. The rest of the team joined in. The ice was broken and the other guys introduced themselves to the new hotshot.

I stayed quiet. Tanner turned and looked at me, his smile fading a little. "You must be Cody. Coach has told me a lot about you. I hear you've been number one."

I nodded. *And it's going to stay that way*, I thought.

"Well, don't be surprised if things change now that I'm on the team."

Coach Wilson stood next to Tanner, still grinning. He looked proud to have him join the team. "Tanner's going to attend the Sports Academy in the fall — that special school for athletes in Calgary. It looks like we're going to be neighbours, too. His parents bought the big house down the street from me."

Great. Now Coach will be spending tons of time with this new kid at the club *and* at home. He'll probably give him a ride every day. The new kid will get more and more of Coach's attention and we'll get less and less. I didn't like where this was going.

Tanner pulled his kayak out of the water, smoothly flipped it up onto his beefy left shoulder, and strode up to the boathouse.

"I'm going to take Tanner up to the boathouse and

show him the ropes," Coach said. "He just flew in yesterday, and he wanted to get out on the water right away, so he hasn't had time to settle in yet. You guys get your boats ready. I'll be back for our regular training session."

Logan, Nick, Nate, Kai, and I started doing our warm-up exercises on the dock while we waited for Coach Wilson to return.

"Tanner seemed like a nice guy," Kai said, stretching.

"And funny, too," Nate laughed.

"He's going to be good to have on the team," Nick added.

Kai, Nick, and Nate went to the other end of the dock to put on their lifebelts and left me standing alone with Logan.

I felt rooted to the dock. "Nice . . . funny . . . good? Were they talking about the same guy I just met?" I asked Logan.

"You have to admit the dude was kickin' it out there on the water. If he's that good in a race, we'll have the best team in the country." Logan strapped his lifebelt around his waist. "You should be glad he's here. It's like you always say, we're out there to win." He slipped his boat into the water and folded his limbs into the egg-shaped opening. With a quick nod, he slowly paddled off.

Maybe Logan had nothing to worry about. He was

just happy to be on the team. He didn't care if he came in second, or even third place. But I liked to win. I had always been the best bantam paddler at the club. Was that all about to change, just because of some hotshot new guy from Toronto? Maybe everyone thought that having a little friendly competition on the team would be good. Thing was, I wasn't sure how friendly it was going to be.

# 5 TABLE FOR TWO

I looked at the clock — 6:30. I had just settled in to do some night-before test cramming at one of the empty tables in the Blue Water Café. On school nights I often stopped by the café after kayak practice. The Blue Water was just down the shoreline from the kayak club. I'd do an hour or two of math, social studies, or language arts and then I'd throw my bike in the back of the pickup truck and Mom would drive us home. When Dad was away on the lookout for forest fires I ate dinner here, too. Gus, the chef who ran the place, made awesome lasagna, and the strawberry cheesecake was ace.

Mom had left for a few minutes to drive to the drugstore in town. She had complained of a headache and needed some pain killers. I knew why. Everybody at the café was worried sick about the rumour of the developers coming in. It's not that everyone was anti-progress here, or anything like that, but we just didn't want our small town to lose the best view of the lake. Mom knew Gus didn't want to sell, but said "everyone has his price." She didn't know how long he could hold out for. If Gus sold, mom would be out of a job, just like all the other staff at the café.

The welcoming bell rang as the heavy wooden door of the café shut. I looked up from my book and glanced at the counter to see who'd just come in. A girl in a tank top stood with her back to me. The blond hair streaming out from under her ball cap seemed familiar.

"Your order will be up in a minute," Gus said. "Why don't you have a seat while you wait?"

The girl spun around like she was doing a 180 and it only took me a split second to remember where I'd seen her before — the skatepark.

She saw me, and her face broke into a smile. "Hey. Haven't I bumped into you some place before?" she said.

My mouth went dry and my lips wouldn't move.

She bounded over to my table and slid into the chair across from me. "You own this place or something?" she joked, nodding at the pages of math and the calculator spread out on the table in front of me.

"No, I'm waiting for my mom — she works here." I struggled to get the words out. "I'm Cody . . . by the way." I was sure I was sounding like a dork.

"Tania," she said, holding out her hand for me to shake. She had the biggest brown eyes I'd ever seen. "That's sweet, about your mom. I hardly ever get to see my mom. She's always working. So's my dad. I'm just here picking up some food to bring home. They never cook."

My mind went blank. A few seconds ticked off the clock. I tried to think of something to say. "Where did you learn to skate?"

"Oh, I've been skating ever since I can remember," Tania said. "I've gone in a few competitions back east, but mostly I do it for kicks."

"You're the best girl skater I've ever seen."

Tania's face froze and she stared me down. "You mean the best *skater* you've ever seen."

"Umm . . . Yeah, that's what I meant, er, mean," I fumbled.

I was relieved when Tania laughed.

"Lasagna dinner for two, to go!" Gus called from the cash register.

"I've got to bounce," Tania said, standing up.

"Enjoy the lasagna," I said, fighting to keep it cool. "It's got the official Cody seal of approval."

"Then I know it'll taste good," she said, waving goodbye while passing my mom, who was just arriving back at the café.

"Who was that?" Mom asked, taking Tania's place in the chair in front of me.

"No one," I said, giving Mom my best quit-bugging-me look.

"She was cute."

"You think so? I hadn't really noticed," I lied, starting

to gather my books. "She hangs out at the skatepark."

"Seems like she likes you," Mom teased.

I didn't care how far it was to get home. I would have done anything at that moment to get away from Mom and her prying. I grabbed my backpack and was halfway out of my seat when Gus came out of the kitchen. "I'm glad you're back, Kate," he said in a serious voice, which was unusual for him. He was almost always happy. "I'm gathering up the staff for a meeting at seven o'clock. 'Fraid I've got some bad news."

Bad news was nothing I wanted to stick around for.

"Don't worry about me, Mom. I'll just ride home," I told her.

"Oh, thanks, Cody. I'm not sure what time we'll be done here," she said, looking both scared and nervous.

"I'll leave the front porch light on for you," I said as I left.

# 6 ALL WET

"Listen up," Coach Wilson commanded as we gathered on the dock early Saturday morning for practice. He liked to set out the plan for each day's training before we headed out onto the water. "In the next three hours we're going to practise our paddling stroke."

"When we're on the water I want everyone to watch how Tanner does it," Coach said, patting a smiling Tanner on the back. "He has perfect technique."

I shot a glance over at Logan and rolled my eyes. I thought he would roll his eyes right back or at least raise an eyebrow in disbelief, but he was buying every word. Logan was staring at Tanner like he was the best kayaker in the world. I looked around the group, and so was everyone else. *I'm just as good as Tanner,* I thought. *Why isn't Coach telling everyone to watch me?*

Coach Wilson asked Tanner to get in his blue kayak and give us a demonstration. Tanner slid into the cockpit of his single-person K-1 and began stroking through the water.

"See how Tanner sits up straight and leans slightly forward," explained Coach. "He holds the paddle above his head, and when he strokes on the left side he keeps his left arm straight and puts the blade into the water as close to the kayak as possible. Fantastic."

Coach Wilson wasn't finished with Tanner's A-plus report card. "Now I want everyone to get in line and follow Tanner out into the lake so we can practise what we've just seen."

*Tanner this and Tanner that.* I had heard enough Tanners for one day. I paddled hard and tucked in right behind him to make sure he knew who was on his tail. Coach and Tanner might think I was number two, but that didn't mean I had to.

Tanner turned around to face me. "Hey, back off!" he shouted. "You shouldn't be closer than one boat length!" I glared back at him and kept on paddling. Logan fell in behind me, followed by Kai, Nick, and Nate with Coach Wilson taking up the rear.

"You look like a baby duck quacking after his mother," Logan kidded.

"Then that makes you the ugly duckling," I shot back. I was in no mood for nursery-rhyme jokes, even from Logan. Coach allowed us to break formation and paddle by ourselves. I didn't waste any time digging my blade into the water and swerving in the other direction from Tanner and Logan.

Even though I was off by myself practising my

paddling technique, I could still see Coach Wilson keeping his eye on Tanner. He was nodding and shouting encouragement at him: "That's the way, Tanner! Pull all the way through the stroke."

After heaping praise on his new star pupil, Coach left Tanner and started paddling toward the other guys. At first I thought he was going to give some advice to Nick or Nate like he usually does. They had joined the club after Logan, Kai, and me, and still had a lot to learn. But he launched his paddle into the water and made a sharp left turn so he was pointing right at me.

"Cody, you're bent too far forward, sit up straight," he scolded.

"I *am* sitting up straight," I complained. But Coach wasn't finished.

"When I tell you to do something I expect you to do it," he said. "The last time I checked, I was the Coach and you were the bantam still learning. So shape up or ship out back to the dock. There won't be any attitude on this team."

Coach had never lectured me like that, not even when I first started lessons. It was like all of a sudden I was doing everything wrong and he wanted to make sure everyone else knew it.

My face burned red, partly because I was mad and partly because I was embarrassed. Coach paddled away. I could see Logan and the other guys staring at me. They all kept their mouths shut and paddled just like the coach had ordered.

"Hey, rookie!" A voice came from behind me. I twisted around in my cockpit to see it was Tanner. "First time in a kayak?" He started to laugh at me. "I thought you were going to be competition for me, Cody, but I was wrong. You're just a poser. You have no idea what you're doing. I'm amazed you haven't tipped over yet."

I dug my paddle into the water, turning my boat so I was right beside Tanner. "I never tip over."

"Wanna bet?" Tanner threatened.

In a flash Tanner was spearing the side of my kayak with the long black blade of his paddle. I was in trouble. The edge of my thin boat started to flip over. I reached my blade out across the water trying to brace myself, but it was no use. The kayak kept rolling over and I crashed headfirst into the freezing water. I was trapped upside-down in my kayak! I needed air, but I didn't know which way was up. I let go of my paddle and pushed my legs out of the cockpit. I couldn't hold my breath much longer. I popped up to the surface like a cork and took a huge gulp of air. Icy waves splashed up against my face and I watched Tanner mocking me as he paddled away. I clenched my fist and punched the water in anger.

From a distance, I could see Coach Wilson turn his kayak toward me. He was waving his arms, signaling for the powerboat to swing by and pick me up. Jason, one of the other coaches, was manning the boat for our practice. I could see him struggling to get the boat's motor to start again. The powerboat was old and kind of crappy, but in situations like this we were glad we had it.

"What's going on?" Coach asked, coming over. I knew he hadn't seen Tanner spear my boat, so he would think I dumped on my own. Nick and Nate were there for the whole thing so I figured they'd back me up.

"You guys quit fooling around or someone is going to get hurt," Coach said, first glaring at me then at Logan, Nick, Nate, and Kai. "Get in the boat, Cody," Coach said. "Your day is done."

My teammates looked down without saying a word and slowly stroked away.

# 7 WHAT'S THE DEAL?

I squinted one eye and reached over to check the time on my iPod — 7:13. *Ugh!* Most Sunday mornings I slept in a lot later. It was the one day of the week I got to be lazy. This morning was different. I had tossed and turned all night and now I lay in bed feeling tired, confused, and sore. Things just weren't making sense. I didn't know what to make of Logan and my other so-called friends not telling Coach that Tanner had tipped me into the water. I didn't know why Mom had been so quiet the last two days. I guess she wasn't ready to talk about the "bad news" yet, not until Dad got home. And my legs felt as stiff as boards from yesterday's two-kilometre run.

It was difficult to decide what I was more ticked about — Tanner spearing the side of my boat, or Logan, Nick, Nate, and Kai not saying anything to Coach. When we'd all arrived back at the boathouse after yesterday's practice, Coach had gathered us together to announce that the Canadian National Regatta would be held at our club next month. We were expected to make a good showing. The only way to do that was to be in top physical condition, so he set out a training plan for the next few weeks.

Man, I thought we were in good condition already. We'd been out on the water for two hours every day after school — longer on Saturdays. My arms always felt like rubber by the end of the week. How much more could we do?

Now Coach had added dry-land training to our schedule. He said the best kayakers from across Canada would be coming and they'd all be in great shape. Just what I needed — more competition.

Then Coach had asked us what another muscle was that we needed to get in shape, besides our arms. None of us knew the answer. I thought it might be some secret kayaking muscle I hadn't heard about. Know-it-all Tanner had piped up, "It's your heart." Still wet from tipping and trying to show him up, I'd laughed and blurted, "There's no way the heart is a muscle!" But then Coach had nodded and said, "Tanner got it right."

*I can't win,* I thought, rolling over in bed and reaching for my PSP.

Mom called down the hall, "Pancakes are on, Cody!"

I dragged myself out of bed, pulled on my shorts and T-shirt, and limped into the kitchen. Dad must have got home early this morning. He was putting glasses of orange juice on the table while Mom was by the stove pouring batter onto a hot frying pan. She looked tired and was still wearing her purple bathrobe.

"I have some news," Mom said. "I wanted to tell you driving home in the truck last night, but you seemed upset enough about practice."

Mom put a stack of pancakes in front of me and slumped down on a chair. "Gus has sold the Blue Water to the golf course developers from the city. He said it was the hardest decision he had ever made in the twenty years he ran the place. He'd been holding out for months, but every time he said no, they offered him more money. Finally, they offered him so much he couldn't refuse. Gus is getting on in years and he's ready to retire. He said this was the only way he could do it. He told us how sorry he was." Mom wiped a tear from her eye. "The café will shut down in two weeks and then it'll be bulldozed to the ground."

"It's a real shame," Dad said, putting a hand on Mom's shoulder. "The Blue Water has been a landmark around here for years."

"I don't know why things can't stay the same for everyone to enjoy," Mom said.

Dad jumped in. "You build a private golf course and the only people who can enjoy those lake views are those that can afford it." I knew where this kind of talk would lead. Dad was a firm believer that nature should be enjoyed by everyone, which was why he worked so hard in his job to make sure that it was protected and looked after.

I didn't feel very hungry hearing their talk. Leaving the last bite of pancake, I got up and carried my plate to the dishwasher.

"Oh, Cody, before I forget," Mom said, "Logan phoned last night after you'd fallen asleep to say that he was probably meeting Nick, Nate, and Kai at the skatepark this morning."

"Oh, right . . . maybe I'll meet up with them later," I said. "Right now I'm going for a run — Coach's orders." I left Mom and Dad to their discussion about the café and headed out.

My sore legs were going to take a while to loosen up so I started jogging slow and easy like Coach had said. I thought I'd take the path around the lake and past the café toward the club. It would be weird not having that old blue building around anymore. It seemed like I'd been there every day of my life. I wondered what would happen to the trail once the Blue Water was gone and the golf course was being built. I knew there would be giant bulldozers, graders, and other heavy equipment carving out the eighteen holes. All the fields and trees would look like a construction war zone. At least the kayaking club was safe . . . for now.

Taking the trail also meant I would avoid the path that lead to the skatepark. I could live without seeing Logan, Nick, Nate, and Kai for a day. I'm sure Tanner would be there with his new buddies.

I decided that after my run, I'd swing by the gym at

the boathouse and lift some weights. The competition at the regatta was going to be tough. When I saw Tanner flexing his biceps yesterday, I knew I was going to have to get stronger if I had any chance of beating him or any of the paddlers from the other provinces.

I picked up my pace. Just thinking about Mr. Perfect Tanner ticked me off. I gritted my teeth and ran faster. At the fork in the path I turned toward the club.

"Wait up, Cody!" a girl's voice called from behind. I twisted my neck and kept running. It was Tania, speeding up the path on a mountain bike.

"Nice wheels," I said, slowing to a jog. The words came more easily now that I was out exercising and not cooped up in the café.

Tania's hair spilled out from her helmet and her eyes twinkled. "It's a sweet ride — carbon frame and full suspension."

"I thought you'd be skating at the park today."

"I was, but then a pack of guys moved in," she said. "Nick, Nate, and the rest of your crew were down there grinding it up this morning."

"You always seem to be out doing something," I said to her.

"No point being home by myself," Tania said. "Even though it's Sunday, Mom and Dad are at the office finishing up some big real estate deal they've been working on."

There was a pause in the conversation. I knew *what*

I wanted to say next, but not *how* to say it.

"Well, I gotta fly," Tania called, the wheels of her bike already spinning.

"Hey, wait," I called. I don't know where I got the nerve, but I knew I had to do it before she was gone. "Want to get together some time?"

She turned on her bike and looked back at me. I saw her nod her head before calling out, "Sure." Then she sped away.

I ran the rest of the way to the club, feeling a lot better than I had earlier.

# 8 CHOKE

The weight room was upstairs in the boathouse. I hadn't gone in there very often because it was usually filled with older teenagers and adults. They'd be sitting at the big metal machines pushing the weights with their arms or legs. I figured weight training must work. Some of those guys had muscles like superheroes. All that was missing were their capes.

The room had six different weight stations. Coach had explained that you pushed the metal weights on some of the machines to make your legs stronger and others to strengthen your upper body. The bench press was for your chest, arms, and shoulders. That was important for kayaking because you counted on all three every time your paddle stroked through the water.

I couldn't lift like the bigger guys. I only slid one-kilogram discs on each end of the bar. They were puny weights, but the bar weighed twenty kilograms just by itself! So, all together I was bench-pressing twenty-two kilograms over my head. Man, it was heavy! I did a couple of reps and then took a quick glance in the mirror. I was hoping to see tennis-ball muscles popping out of the top of my biceps, but so far they still looked like marshmallows. I didn't quite have that Hulk look I was going for. I guessed it would just take time. I can see how strong Coach Wilson is and I know he spent a ton of hours in the weight room while training for the Canadian team.

I grabbed my water bottle and headed back to the locker room to fill it up at the fountain. When I was coming back into the weight room, I heard the chants.

"Eighteen . . . nineteen . . . twenty!"

*Something must be going on,* I thought. I pushed through the door and saw Logan's frizzy red hair sticking up among a dozen other heads crowded around the bench press at the far end. What was everyone doing here? They were huddled so tightly together I couldn't make out who was pumping the iron. I rushed up and peeked over Nate's shoulder to get a better look. *Tanner.* I should have known.

"Cody!" Logan shouted. "We were all down at the skatepark when Tanner dared any of us to take him on in the weight room."

Tanner sat up on the padded bench to take a break from doing his reps. He had been lying down with his back on the bench and his head and chest underneath the steel bar that rested on a stand above him. I could see by the smirk on his face that he was digging all the attention. He'd already pushed up the metal bar with two black iron weights on each end twenty times. The most reps I'd ever done was ten, but I wasn't about to tell anyone. I doubt whether Nick, Nate, or Kai could do many more. And I knew Logan and his spaghetti arms couldn't for sure.

"One . . . two . . . three . . ." Tanner was at it again. I looked to see how much weight he was pushing and expected it to be two kilograms like Coach Wilson had recommended. *What the?* There was a round five-kilo weight on each end of the bar!

Tanner sat up, took a sip from his water bottle, and stared at the faces still frozen in awe of his weightlifting. "Anybody want to take me on?"

Everyone shook his head. Nobody was as ripped as Tanner.

"Hey, Logan, how about you? You're the weakest excuse for a paddler I've ever seen. You're so tall and skinny you even look like a paddle."

I could see Logan's face burn red, but I knew he wouldn't put up a fight. Logan may not have been the strongest guy in the world, but it didn't matter. He was one of the funniest. Even though I was still mad at Logan for not sticking up for me yesterday, I couldn't let Tanner rip into my best friend like that.

I took a step forward. "Maybe I will."

"You, Cody? You're joking, right? Even though I'm

wasted from working out, I can still take you," Tanner boasted.

"Let's find out," I shot back.

"Who's going to spot for us?" Tanner asked, looking up at Logan's bony frame. "I won't need you but Cody will, big time. What about it, stick-man?"

Logan screwed up his face at being called a name, but he nodded and stepped behind the bench-press bar.

"How much iron does a wimp like you think I can press?" Tanner asked, trying to stare me down.

I didn't want to seem like a complete slacker so I picked the same weight Tanner had just been lifting, even though it was more than I had ever pushed in my life. Maybe Tanner would be so worn out he would back down. "How about five kilograms on each end?"

"Don't be a wuss!" Tanner laughed. "Hey, stick-man, put on two of those ten-kilogram babies."

I quickly did the math in my head: 20kg + 10kg + 10kg = 40kg. That was almost as much as I weighed. There was no way I could lift that much!

My heart started pounding as I watched Tanner lie on the bench and slide under the shiny steel bar. Logan stood ready to grab the bar in case it was too heavy for him to lift by himself. He didn't believe Tanner could push it back up either.

Word of the dare spread like wildfire around the club. More kids cruised into the weight room. The growing crowd of spectators tightened their ring around the action like a noose. The coaches were in a meeting downstairs. There was no one to interfere.

Tanner raised his arms. His hands grabbed the bar a shoulder's width apart. He took two deep breaths. *Huh! Huh!* Then with one last noisy grunt he pushed up to release the bar from the stand and lowered it down to his chest. Now he had to push the bar back up to the stand. That would count as one. Tanner gathered all his strength. His face turned blood red. His bent arms flexed. He pushed up with all his might and the bar slowly lifted off his chest. His arms became straighter and straighter until finally he was able to place the bar back on the stand. He'd done it! Logan stared down in amazement. I couldn't believe it either and stood there in silence. It was my turn next.

"Nothing to it," smiled Tanner, standing up from the bench and slapping his hands together.

He turned to Logan. "You better get ready, bean-pole."

I lay on the bench and slid under the bar. I could feel the adrenaline starting to rush through my body. I felt stronger than I had ever felt before. I could do this! I raised my arms and grabbed the bar. I pushed up and the steel bar lifted. *Yes!* But then it came crashing down on my chest. The weight was crushing. I struggled to push it up. My arms strained. My cheeks filled with air. I grunted. I groaned. I gasped. It was no use. I was trapped under forty kilograms of iron and steel. Logan thrust his hands out and tried to pull the bar off, but he was too weak. Tanner must have known he wouldn't be strong enough. The bar held me prisoner. It was like a vice clamped around my chest and it was starting to squeeze. I couldn't breath. I couldn't move. I started to choke.

Suddenly, the door to the weight room burst open.

"Coach Wilson!" Logan yelled in surprise.

"What's going on?" Coach shouted, pushing his way through the crowd to the bench press where I was pinned. "Logan, pull the bar off Cody! Nick, you better help him!"

"Uuuggghhh." I sat up gagging.

"You okay, Cody?" Coach asked, looking concerned.

I nodded, taking in deep breaths.

"Good."

But then Coach's face turned fierce. "Now listen to me, Cody, Tanner, and the rest of you. This is why we have rules. This is why we don't fool around. This is why one day someone is going to get hurt. That day was almost today. You guys know better than to lift weights that are too heavy. We've been over this before." He pointed his finger at us to make sure we remembered each point.

"Tanner started it —" I began in self-defence.

"I don't care how it started. But I'll tell you how it's going to end. Neither one of you will be allowed in the weight room for the next month." Coach Wilson gave one final stern look at Tanner and me, then stomped out. We were left staring at one another in silence.

# 9 AUSSIE TIME

The boathouse was buzzing that Friday after practice. Logan had overheard some of the coaches talking after training yesterday while he was putting away his kayak. He had snuck his way through the racks to get as close to the huddled coaches as he could without being seen. Logan was the perfect listening spy. His ears were bigger than normal and stood out from his head like a couple of satellite dishes. Now he was passing on what he heard to me. It was a rumour. And it was big.

"Cody, I think there might be a sleepover here at the club tomorrow night," he said keeping his voice low like a secret agent.

I looked at him in surprise. There'd never been a sleepover at the kayak club before. Why would there be one now? It's not like you can take boats out after dark. It's way too dangerous.

"What's going on?" I whispered. "Is it someone's birthday?"

"Nothing small like that. This is huge, dude!" Logan

said excitedly while spreading his long arms far apart to show just how big the secret was.

"Spill it," I demanded.

"You know how the Global Kayak Championships are taking place this weekend?" started Logan.

"Yeah."

"And you know how the finals are being held to-morrow?"

"Yeah, and?"

"We're having a sleepover in the boathouse to watch them!" he blurted, unable to hold the secret in any longer.

"That's awesome," I whispered. "But how come we have to watch them at night?"

"Because the Globals are in Australia, dude," Logan explained.

"I knew that."

"That's like down under on the other side of the freakin' world," Logan said.

"I knew that, too."

"And sixteen hours ahead of our time," Logan said.

"That part I didn't know," I said, shaking my head.

Logan smiled a toothy grin and hit me with a time zone quiz. "So, if the K-1 race is scheduled for *tomorrow* at four o'clock in the afternoon in Sydney, what time is it here?"

Now I wished I had my calculator. I scratched my head and subtracted sixteen hours from four o'clock in my head to get the answer. "That means the race would take place at . . . midnight *tonight* here."

"You got it!" Logan said, impressed that I wasn't a complete dolt and could figure it out. "I heard the coaches say that all we have to do is get our parents to sign a permission slip . . ."

I hoped Logan's mom would agree. Ever since his dad split two years ago she hadn't let him do anything by himself. Or at least that's the way it seemed. She drove him everywhere except school. When he first started kayak lessons she would sit and wait in the car the whole time he was out on the water. For three hours every morning! Now she just drops him off and goes shopping or something, so I guess things are getting better. I think Logan likes being at the club more than being at home where he gets kind of lonely. I mean, there's only so much PlayStation you can play. He has a lot of friends here. Sometimes, I think we take the place of his dad.

I was pretty sure my Mom and Dad would say yes to the sleepover. Mom's sadness over losing the café had turned to anger, and now she and Dad were too busy trying to come up with ways to halt the development of the area around the café to say no. The only problem was that I had arranged to meet Tania at the skatepark after practice so we could hang out. I hadn't told Logan or anyone else that I liked her. And, as busy as Mom and Dad had been, I was pretty sure they'd notice if I didn't come home at all tonight.

Logan noticed my hesitation. "Umm, dude?" he said, waving a hand in front of my face. "What's going on in there?"

"Nothing," I said. "It's just that I . . . well, I . . . I was going to meet someone after practice tonight."

"Someone? Who?"

"Well, umm . . . a friend . . . a girl I know."

"Friend? Girl? A date? You have a date!" Logan yelled. I quickly clamped my hand over his mouth.

"Shush," I demanded. "I don't want the whole world to know." I removed my hand from Logan's mouth.

"Who's the lucky girl?" Logan said mockingly.

"No one. Just someone I met at the skatepark the other day."

"Girl . . . at the skatepark? You don't mean Tania, the new girl?"

I smiled and looked down.

"Cody, man, don't you know who she is? She's — " But before Logan could finish, the coaches interrupted by saying that they had an announcement to make.

"This is it!" Logan said excitedly. Thankfully, my date with Tania was forgotten for the moment.

★ ★ ★

When I got to the boathouse around ten that night, Nick, Nate, Kai, and Logan were joking around outside. Their sleeping bags were stacked on a nearby wooden bench, and I threw mine on top of the pile. Parents were there dropping off other kids, too.

I thought about earlier that evening when I'd been hanging out with Tania. We'd decided to bike back to my place to hang out there and get my parents to sign the permission form for the sleepover. We had played basketball on the driveway and then some video games. She liked to play a lot of sports, like me. She wasn't always in it to win, but she could sure hold her own. When it was time for her to go home, my mom had thrown her bike in the back of the truck and driven her, while I stayed home to gather up my stuff for the sleepover.

It felt kind of eerie to be at the kayak club this late at night, and to see the moon glaring off the still lake. The boathouse stood three stories high and was cut into the side of a big hill that sloped down to the edge of the lake. Grey concrete walls held up the roof, which was covered by long sheets of blue metal. The bottom level was where we kept all the boats. There were rows of K-1, K-2, and K-4 kayaks, all resting in special long wooden racks. A collection of paddles were hidden inside a cabinet in the corner. There was a huge garage door that made it easy to move the boats in and out when they had to be carried down to the water.

The second level had two rooms. There was the locker room where we kept our backpacks and the weight room where we pumped iron. Or at least used to pump iron. It was still off limits for another three weeks to Tanner and me. On the top floor there was an eating area and a lounge with big windows that looked out over the lake. After training ended at noon in the summer, we'd eat our lunches at the long tables. It was kind of like being in the school cafeteria. Afterwards the coaches would sometimes show us a kayak training video on the big TV in the lounge or pull out a laptop and show racing clips on YouTube. We'd sit on the comfy couches or lie on the carpeted floor to watch. The lounge was where we were all going to watch the race tonight.

When it looked like everyone had arrived, some of the coaches came and tried to round us all up.

"Let's grab our sleeping bags and head upstairs," I said.

"Last one to the top is a rotten dude!" Logan yelled.

The five members of the original Bantam Sprint Team rushed up the stairs, taking them two at a time. Logan, with his giraffe legs, took them three at a time. We couldn't wait for the kayak finals to start. There was still a bit of time before the first race so there was plenty of time to chill. I looked around the lounge, thankful that Tanner wasn't there. This was shaping up to be an awesome night.

*Aaaarrrppppp!* Logan let out a humungous burp. He had just downed a can of Mountain Dew and was now belching out all twenty-six letters of the alphabet. We had parked ourselves on the couch and were cracking up. Then things got even better. Coach Wilson brought a big bowl of popcorn out from the kitchen and placed it on the table in front of us. "Dig in, guys!" he said, falling into a big leather chair.

"Sweet!" Five pairs of hands grabbed for the fluffy white kernels all at once.

"I bet Australia is a cool place," I said, chewing.

"How would you know?"

I turned around to see that Tanner had snuck up behind us. I groaned inwardly.

"Australia's got all kinds of cool animals," I said. "They've got more deadly creatures than anywhere else in the world. And they have kangaroos. They're a lot tougher than you think. I've seen them at the zoo."

"Yeah, well, I've seen kangaroos in person," Tanner said, looking smug. "And they weren't hopping around any zoo."

"You've been to Australia, dude?" Logan asked.

"Who hasn't?" Tanner said, getting more stuck-up by the minute.

Logan, Nick, Nate, Kai, and I looked wide-eyed at each other. None of us had been to any foreign countries. I think Nick and Nate went to Hawaii for one Christmas vacation, but that was it.

"What was it like?" Kai asked.

Tanner stood looking down at us. "Australia's nothing special. Unless you like swimming in the warm ocean, surfing huge waves, sun tanning on sandy beaches, watching kangaroos running wild, spotting koala bears climbing in eucalyptus trees, snorkeling under the water with a million different coloured tropical fish on the Great Barrier Reef, or having an all-you-can-eat barbecue every night. Oh yeah, and it never gets cold. Other than that it was pretty boring."

"Sounds pretty fly to me," Logan said grinning.

"Yeah, when my sister and I were there last winter visiting relatives, we went in a surfing competition. Tania even placed. It was awesome."

I had zoned out listening to Tanner's travelogue. But that last part got my attention. *Tania? How did he know Tania?* Suddenly, it all made sense. I must have been blind!

# 10 MIDNIGHT MYSTERY

I looked up at the clock. There was still half an hour to go till midnight. I was reeling from finding out that Tania was Tanner's sister. How could they even be related? She was so nice and he was such a jerk. Then I started to put the pieces together. They had almost the same hair colour. They both were athletic. They'd arrived here about the same time. I'd been too preoccupied with year-end exams at school and what was happening with Mom and Dad to notice the connections earlier. I felt like Tanner was ruining my life.

I tried to focus on the TV, which was being switched back and forth between Bart bugging Principal Skinner on *The Simpsons* and Peter being a buffoon on *Family Guy*.

I needed to get out of there for a minute and get some fresh air. I got up from the sofa and wound my way across the floor, being careful not to step on any bodies sprawled out on sleeping bags

I made my way down the stairs to the ground floor.

When I got there, I was surprised to see that the large doors were open. Coach Wilson was standing there, looking out over the water. I thought he would be hanging out with the other coaches.

I walked up beside him and glanced over. He looked more tired than usual tonight. I thought talking about the upcoming Global races might make him feel better.

"The kayaking is going to be wicked," I said. "I hope the Canadian guy wins."

"I hope he does, too," Coach Wilson said. "But things don't always turn out like you plan."

"There's no way he can lose," I said. "He wins almost every race he enters."

Coach let out a long, sad sigh. "I used to think that way, too. But . . ." His voice trailed off.

I leaned in a little. Was I finally going to learn the story of why he didn't make the Canadian Olympic team? I couldn't believe that none of the other guys were here with me. They'd be so jealous when they found out that Coach had told *me*. Hey, maybe Tanner wasn't his favourite after all.

Coach Wilson started to speak in a slow, soft voice: "It doesn't seem that long ago. There was a group of us training hard to make the Canadian Olympic Kayaking Team. We were from different parts of Canada, but we all had one common goal — to be picked for the squad that would compete in Beijing, China. I was probably in the best shape of my life. Every day, I spent

59

six hours out on the water and then I'd hit the weight room for two more to build up my strength. They were long days, but I knew it was worth it. I was eating three squares a day and hitting the sack early to get my sleep. You've got to remember that resting is just as important as exercise.

"The team was going to be decided at the Olympic trials on the same course where the kayaking events took place during the 1976 Montreal Olympics. The organizers of the Canadian Kayaking Team had decided that only one athlete could be selected for each distance. That meant I had to win the 1,000–metre race to make the team. Coming in second place didn't get you anything but a pat on the back and a handshake. I wasn't too concerned. My main rival was Matt Marshall. I had beaten him in every race we had competed in earlier that summer. I was ranked number one in the country and was the favourite to win. There was no way I could lose. Or at least that's what I thought. The race was set for a Saturday afternoon, just like today's Global race is scheduled for Down Under. My plan was to sit back and let Matt do all the hard work. I could relax knowing that I was the stronger kayaker and could pass him whenever I wanted. That was the plan, but it wasn't the way it went down.

"The starting horn went off and my paddle splashed into the water. Normally I would dig hard right away to get up to maximum speed, but that day I didn't hit the gas pedal. I just sped up slowly. There was no need to rush. Matt was two lanes over and I could see him out of the corner of my eye. His blades flashed through the water with a fury I hadn't seen before and he had shot into the lead. He looked determined, but I still wasn't worried. I sat back and waited for him to get tired. At the halfway point of the race I was still chasing Matt, but we had moved out in front of the pack. The other four kayakers didn't have the strength to keep up and had fallen behind. It was just the two of us skimming between the yellow markers to the finish line 500 metres away. Matt looked powerful. He was paddling at a hundred strokes per minute. I didn't think he could keep up that blazing pace. I waited for his arms to burn out. That would be my chance to strike. But what happened next shocked me.

"Instead of slowing down, Matt shifted into a higher gear and sped up! I looked over at him twice to double-check his pace. He started to pull away from me. I couldn't relax any longer. I thrust my paddles into the water and cranked up my pace. I was in panic mode. My strokes weren't as smooth as they should have been and my blades were kicking up white splash on both sides of my boat. I was losing my form but it was too late to care. With only a hundred metres to go I put the hammer down and gave it everything I had. Now I was paddling at 120 strokes a minute. I had never paddled so fast — not even in training. I started to gain on Matt.

I thought it was going to be enough and I would catch him before the finish. I thought the end would be just like I had planned.

"The big red buoys that marked the finish line were now in our sights. My heart was pounding so hard I thought it was going to jump out of my chest. I just had to keep up my attack for a few seconds more. But I couldn't hold my pace. I had waited too long to make my move. No matter how hard I paddled, I couldn't close the gap. Matt was still a full boat-length ahead of me. The horn blared to announce that the winning paddler had crossed the finish line. That was Matt. A second later the horn sounded again. This time it was for my boat coming in second place. I was beat. My body sagged forward as I tried to force air into my oxygen-starved lungs. Even though I was dead tired all I could think about were those two words — *second place*. I wasn't going to make the Canadian Olympic team and there would be no trip to Beijing. I was crushed. Matt had paddled the race of his life and deserved to win."

Coach Wilson fixed his gaze on me. I listened, not even wanting to blink.

"I made a mistake no athlete should make. I thought no one could beat me. But no one is unbeatable. The race was over, but I still couldn't believe I had lost. I sat in my kayak drifting alone out on the water for a few minutes, wondering what had happened.

"Over the years I've replayed that race a thousand times in my head. And you know what? I still haven't won it yet."

Coach Wilson grinned, knowing he would never win the race no matter how many times he relived it. I knew deep down he wasn't smiling at all.

# 11 PADDLE BATTLE

"Nova Scotia, New Brunswick, Quebec, Ontario . . ." Coach Wilson held his clipboard and began reading out the provinces sending competitors to the Canadian Kayak Championships. ". . . Manitoba, Saskatchewan, Alberta, and British Columbia," he said, completing his Atlantic-to-Pacific list.

It was the first Monday after school ended. Every member of our club was gathered outside the boathouse to hear the announcement. "There will be over 500 of the best male and female kayakers coming from across the country," he said proudly. "And they'll all be coming right here to Ghost Lake."

The big national regatta was only five days away. We'd have the advantage of knowing the winds and the waves on our own lake. Plus, we could sleep in our own beds at night and not have to stay in some strange hotel with lumpy mattresses.

The coaches wanted the club to look spotless. There were a million things to do and everyone at the club had to chip in to help. There'd be no slackers — not even Logan. We cleaned up the boathouse from top to bottom: vacuuming the lounge, sweeping the kitchen, and even scrubbing the toilets! Then we made a gigantic banner to greet the teams when they arrived. First, we laid a long white strip of paper out on the ground. Then we each drew a huge letter that was part of the message. I used a big brush to paint a bright red "C" that must have been a metre high. When we finished, two of the coaches stood on ladders and hung the banner over the garage door of the boathouse: *Welcome Canada's Best Kayakers!*

Every kayaker in Canada was counting down the days to the national regatta. It was the big monster event of the year. It was nerve-wracking because it was also the biggest challenge of the year. Months of training would be put on the line in every race. Each athlete would be in peak condition for the competition.

Kayakers weren't the only ones getting their tickets for Calgary. There would be hundreds of coaches, parents, brothers, and sisters all here to cheer on their teams. Some would drive by car and some would fly by plane. The place would be crawling with people! Not to mention all the kayaks. Before leaving their home city each team would load their boats onto long trailers and have them towed to Calgary behind powerful pickup trucks. It would take a week to drive all the way across the country from Halifax!

We knew the names of the kayakers who would represent each province, but there was still one big question. Who would be chosen to represent our province? Who would be picked for the Alberta team?

Coach Wilson was on it. "To get us ready for the national regatta we're going to have a club regatta of our own," he said to the group of eager faces. "There will be races in every age group to determine who qualifies for the Alberta team and the right to compete in the championship this weekend."

*No sweat*, I thought to myself. As long as I came first, second, or third I should qualify for the K-1 event. I started to walk away, thinking I was a shoo-in to make the bantam team. Besides, it would be the perfect excuse for me to keep avoiding Tania. Ever since the night of the sleepover, my mom had been drilling me non-stop about her, and I needed an excuse to stay out of the house now that summer vacation had started.

"I have one more important announcement," Coach Wilson said loudly. I stopped dead in my tracks. "Only the winner of the K-1 race will qualify. As a consolation prize, the second place finisher will join the winner in the K-2 race."

Logan came running up. "What are you going to do, dude?"

"What do you mean?"

"There's only one way to qualify for the K-1 race!" Logan said.

"I've got two ears. I heard him."

"You have to straight-up beat Tanner!" Logan exclaimed.

"Whatever. No problem."

"Are you kidding me, dude? You haven't beat him yet. He's owned you!" Logan seemed more flipped out than I was about the race.

"There's always a first time. No one is unbeatable." I heard the words come out of my mouth, but I wasn't quite sure even I believed them.

* * *

Logan and I stood in front of the bulletin board to check the race schedule posted by Coach Wilson. I ran my finger down the list to find the start time for the K-1 bantam boys 1000-metre sprint.

"There it is," Logan said. "Two o'clock on the nose."

That was only an hour away.

"We better find the other guys and get ready," I said.

Logan and I walked into the boathouse. Nick, Nate, and Kai were already inside pulling their blue, green, and white kayaks out of the wooden racks. Next they'd carry the boats down to the dock to "whip-in." Before a big race like this you had to "whip-in," or check in, with an official to get your lane number and matching bib number that you tied over your T-shirt.

I went over to the paddle cabinet to get my trusty

blade, the same one I'd been using since I started at the club. But for some reason it wasn't there. I didn't know who had taken it, but I had my suspicions. *Whatever*, I thought. I'd just use another one. *How different could a paddle be?*

I threw the new paddle inside my red kayak and carried it safely out of the boathouse before flipping it onto my shoulder. *I wonder where Tanner is?* I said to myself. *Probably alone in a quiet place planning how he's going to beat me.* Boy was I wrong! Sitting on a bench straight ahead of me was Tanner, chewing a big wad of gum and reading a comic book. If he was worried, he sure wasn't showing it.

Tanner looked up. "Good luck, Cody," he said, mocking me. "You're going to need it." He burst a big pink bubble. "Oh yeah, and one more thing, stay away from my sister!"

Steaming mad, I carried my kayak down to the dock. I hadn't had any contact at all with Tania since finding out she was Tanner's sister. I had no idea how or when he'd found out that we'd hung out at my place last week.

The battle for first place hadn't begun yet. Tanner seemed as though he couldn't care less about his race with me. In his mind he had already won. I'd trained harder this week than ever before. He was in for the race of his life.

I tossed my boat into the water beside the dock,

braced my paddle across the front of the cockpit, and slid my legs into the hole. I checked to make sure my lifebelt was snug around my waist and my numbered bib was tied tightly around my chest. I didn't want it flying off in the middle of the race. I gave a rough push off the dock with my blade and started paddling out to the start area in the middle of the lake. *Let's do this,* I said to myself.

Logan, Nick, Nate, and Kai were ahead of me, but there was no Tanner in sight. For all I knew he was still reading his stupid comic book. It would serve him right if he missed the race.

"Coming through, kayak clown!" It was Tanner paddling hard and passing me on the left. "I gave you a head start and you still can't beat me to the starting line," he mocked.

*Knock yourself out,* I thought. If Tanner wanted to use up his energy before the race, he could go ahead. I was going to save mine.

Coach Wilson was the official starter for the race. He sat in the powerboat that bobbed up and down in the water at one end of the starting line. Tanner, Logan, Nick, Nate, Kai, and I all paddled into our lanes. We gently feathered the water back and forth with our blades to keep our boats even across the imaginary line.

The sun blazed down from high in the afternoon sky. A light breeze blew small ripples across the lake. I spun my ball cap around and took a quick glance to my left. It was Tanner. He was in the lane next to me. He turned his head and gave me a stare that was half smile and half sneer. The look on his face said, *you don't stand a chance.* At least I wouldn't have to look far to see the enemy.

*Brrraaarrr!* Coach Wilson blew the horn and we blasted off. I took a deep breath and plunged my paddle hard into the deep blue water. My kayak shot forward. White curls of water churned beside my boat. I focused my eyes straight ahead. I could check on Tanner later.

I kept my pace cranked up. *Stroke . . . stroke . . . stroke.* My strategy was simple. I thought the only way I could win was to go all out right from the start. I had tossed and turned in bed all last night planning my strategy. I had to get out front and stay out front. I didn't want to sit back and fall behind. I could still hear Coach Wilson's voice in my head. *"I made a mistake no athlete should make. I thought no one could beat me."* That's not what I thought. I knew Tanner could beat me. He always beat me! I was the underdog. No one expected me to win. Not Tanner, not Coach Wilson, not even Logan. But I would prove them wrong. I dug in.

*Thump . . . thump.* My heart pounded in my chest. Adrenaline shot into my muscles. A full minute passed before I settled into a rhythm. My breaths and strokes started to work together. *Stroke . . . stroke . . . breathe. Stroke . . . stroke . . . breathe.* I began to feel more relaxed. My shoulders and arms pulled the blades through the water, first on the left, then on the right. My kayak skimmed along the top of the water. I was flying! I don't think I had ever paddled so fast.

At the halfway point of the race I still had a slim lead over Tanner. Logan, Nick, Nate, and Kai were being left in our wake. There were 500 metres to go but I felt strong. *I can do this,* I thought. Then I started to wonder. *Why is Tanner still behind me? He's never trailed me before. Is he trying hard? Is he tired? Or is he just sucking me in to let me get ahead on purpose?*

I was heating up. Sweat coated my arms and dripped down my forehead. The salt stung my eyes, but I couldn't wipe it away. I had to keep my hands on the shaft. Even taking a break for a split second would let Tanner rocket by me. I blinked hard and paddled on.

Now the big red buoys that marked the finish line were in sight. I didn't think my heart could pound any faster, but it did. I shot a glance out of the corner of my eye. I still couldn't see the long pointed tip of Tanner's white kayak. That meant he hadn't caught up to me yet. He was still half a boat-length behind. I gripped my paddle and made every stroke as smooth as possible. *Hold on, Cody,* I told myself. I almost couldn't believe I was in the lead. I could win!

There was less than a minute to go. This was the time I had to put the hammer down. Every inch of my body ached, but I couldn't think about the pain. I blocked everything out of my mind except the finish line. Suddenly, I saw a flash of white to my left. It was the bow of Tanner's boat! He was almost even with me!

I panicked. Instead of keeping my stroke rate steady like Coach Wilson always said, I tried to crank it up even faster. My tired arms felt like rubber. My strokes were no longer smooth but out of control. My blades thrashed the water and started to hit the sides of the kayak. *Whack . . . whack . . . whack!* All of a sudden the left side went dead. It didn't feel like I was paddling through water. It felt like I was paddling through air. I looked down and saw my worst nightmare — the left blade had snapped off!

I was only stroking on the right side, which forced my kayak to turn left. I was heading straight for Tanner's lane! If I crossed over the red markers I would be disqualified. The finish was only a few metres away. I could almost touch it. But it was no use. I had to stop paddling. My kayak glided helplessly into Tanner's lane just as he skimmed ahead of me. He held his paddle up high over his head and turned to laugh at me as he crossed the finish line.

I couldn't believe it. It was like a bad dream. I was so close. I didn't know if I would have won, but I never got the chance to find out. All my hard work ruined by a stupid paddle. *Where had it gone, anyway?* I was mad. Mad at Tanner for winning, and mad at myself for losing control and hacking the side of my boat. There would be only one bantam paddler representing

Alberta in the big national K-1 race, and it wasn't me. And to make matters worse, I was going to have to race in the K-2 boat with him. That was no consolation. That was torture.

I lay my broken paddle across the front of the bow and slumped forward, trying to catch my breath. Sweat still dripped down my face but I was too tired to raise my arms and wipe it away. I hung my head. I knew if I looked up Tanner would be celebrating. It was the last thing in the world I wanted to see.

Maybe Coach Wilson was wrong. Maybe some racers were unbeatable. There may have been six of us drifting out there on the water, but I felt like I was the only one. My worn-out muscles would recover. I wasn't so sure about my pride.

# 12 STORM WATCH

*Brrriiinnng!* The phone woke me up. But I didn't care who was calling. Or what the message might be. It was probably just Coach reminding me to come to the club today anyway. Besides, Mom or the machine would get it. I dragged myself out of bed and shuffled down the hall into the kitchen. The radio was playing, but there was no one there. I guess Mom had gone grocery shopping. She knew I was disappointed about losing the race yesterday and she'd made my favourite breakfast to try and cheer me up. She'd also left a note: *Enjoy the pancakes, Cody! Be home soon — Mom.* I poured syrup over the tall stack and sat down to eat. JACK-FM had just finished playing some sappy Miley Cyrus song on the radio when the weather guy came on in a serious low voice.

"A surprise storm is expected to blow through the Calgary area this morning," he said. "One hour of heavy rain and high winds from the mountains are forecast. Thunder and lighting are possible. Caution is advised."

I looked out the window and all I saw was blue sky.

*The weather guy isn't always right,* I thought to myself. *Maybe the storm will miss us.*

Not that it mattered much. I was in no rush to get to the club and hear Tanner gloat over his victory. Before today, I couldn't wait to jump out of bed and get going. But for the first time since I'd took up kayaking, I wasn't in the mood to hit the water. Even though there were still a couple of days to train before the nationals, all I wanted to do was lie on the couch with a big bag of chips and watch TV. Who cared about the K-2 race anyway? Tanner would just screw it up for me. Still, I had to go. Coach would be expecting us to show. I slung my backpack over my shoulder and slunk out the door. I went to grab my bike, but noticed that tire was flat. Of course! What a day this was going to be. I didn't have the energy to hunt around for a patch and an air pump. I would walk to the club today. As I headed down the driveway toward the trail, I noticed that Dad's forestry truck was still here, on a weekday morning. *Weird,* I thought. He and Mom must have gone somewhere together in her truck.

Two joggers ran past me as I trudged along the path. There must have been some special force field holding my feet down because it felt like I was moving in slow motion. My brain was still stuck on the race yesterday. I was jealous Tanner would be the club's only bantam K-1 kayaker entered in the nationals on the weekend. It could have been me: *if only* the race had been a bit shorter, *if only* my paddle hadn't broken, *if only* I had a bigger lead, *if only* my form had been better. Just running through the list in my head made me realize *if only* was a pretty lame excuse.

Still, I wish it was Logan or Nick or Kai — anyone but Tanner. Ever since he moved here from Toronto, Tanner had acted like he was better than everyone else. It wasn't just because he kept winning. That was bad enough. It was because he kept rubbing it in: "Nice try, Cody . . . Better luck next time, Cody . . . Oh, were you even in that race, Cody?"

I was sick of it. Plus, I hated the way he sucked up to the coach: "You're the best, Coach Wilson . . . You sure know your kayaks, Coach Wilson . . . I think Cody needs more coaching than I do, Coach Wilson."

I couldn't wait to cheer on everyone from our club — everyone except Tanner.

My shoulders drooped and I straggled along, staring down at my shoes. Fifteen minutes turned into thirty. As I rounded the last corner to the boathouse I finally looked up. *What was that at the entrance?* I walked down the hill to get a closer look. A big white piece of paper had been tacked to the front door and was flapping in the breeze. I ran up and read the message printed in big letters, "*STORM WARNING — CLUB CLOSED!*" *Man! Why is everyone so choked about the weather?* I said to myself.

I glanced up over the tall trees and got my answer

— big heavy clouds were rolling in from the west. The sky was changing from blue to grey and it was changing fast. I'd been so busy feeling sorry for myself on the walk to the club that I hadn't noticed. A growl of thunder rumbled in the distance. I checked the front door. It was locked so I took a quick look around. There wasn't a coach or kid to be seen. Everyone was staying home because of the forecast. It was a ghost town at Ghost Lake.

I felt the wind pick up and the temperature drop. I pulled my hat down and was rummaging in my bag for a hoodie when I noticed the big garage door was wide open. *Those coaches sure don't lock up very well,* I thought. I scrambled around the side of the boathouse to where the canoes and kayaks were kept. I took a quick peek inside to make sure all the boats were in their racks before I closed the door.

A single kayak was missing — Tanner's white K-1. The boat was sleek and fast but not as stable as some of the other kayaks. Tanner didn't mind if the boat was tippy as long as it sliced through the water. A gust of wind whipped through the trees and marble-sized raindrops started to splatter on the pavement. I guess the weather guy *was* right.

Tanner must have got here early and decided to take his kayak out for one last training workout before his big race on Saturday. But he broke three club rules. One — never paddle alone. Two — always tell a coach you're on the water. And three — never go out in bad weather. Tanner didn't seem to care about rules, though. He thought he was way too good for that.

*Serves him right. That's what you get for not listening.* I pulled down the garage door and started to walk back up the hill. I didn't really want to train today and now I was off the hook. I could go back home and watch TV all day if I felt like it.

*Crraacckk!* A bolt of lightning sizzled in the distance. I watched for another flash and counted to thirty before the thunder rolled over me again. The storm was still in the mountains, but it was headed this way. I had to hurry if I was going to make it home without getting soaked. I got to the top of the hill and took a quick look back. The lake was starting to get choppy and the rain was starting to fall. It wasn't safe to be out on the water — even for an egomaniac like Tanner.

I ran down to the dock. I couldn't see Tanner anywhere. The water was cement grey just like the sky. You couldn't tell where one stopped and the other began. Rain pelted my face, making it almost impossible to see. I scanned the whole lake and all I saw were a few Canada Geese honking as they flew for cover. Even the birds were smart enough to seek shelter.

I knew what I had to do. It didn't matter that I thought Tanner was a big jerk. Or that he had beat me in the race yesterday. I had to forget about all that. He was somewhere out there on the lake. A flash storm was blowing in from the mountains and the waves were splashing higher and higher by the minute. Tanner's life was in danger. No one else knew he had made the stupid decision to take a kayak out there by himself. I had to get help. There was no time to waste. I started running up the hill to get Coach Wilson. Of all the days not to have my bike!

Coach lived about a kilometre from the club. I knew the address of his house because he had invited the whole sprint team over for a barbecue last year. The regular route was to follow the sidewalk along the road. I figured I was in good enough shape to make it. But I couldn't wait another second.

I was just about to take off down the sidewalk when it hit me. I could take a short cut through the park instead! That way I could chop down the distance. I'd have to use every ounce of strength to get there as fast as I could. There could be no letting up. No losing form at the end. This time I wasn't racing to beat Tanner. I was racing to save him.

I kicked into high gear. My feet pounded along the path that followed the edge of the lake. A fierce wind was bending the tall evergreen trees and shaking the branches. When the storm was against me it was like running into an invisible wall. I leaned into the wind, pushing my legs and pumping my arms. When the wind was at my back I felt like I was flying. My legs couldn't spin any faster.

I looked out over the cliff and across the water. Frothy whitecaps were cresting out in the middle of the lake. Closer to the shore waves were crashing against the dock. Cold raindrops continued to pepper my skin. Beads of warm sweat were trickling down my forehead. I was hot and cold at the same time. The rain and the sweat streamed across my face and stung my eyes. I pulled the beak of my hat lower and rushed on.

The end of the park was just ahead. I raced past the empty soccer field, past the baseball diamond and past the swings to where the grass met the sidewalk. A few more blocks and I would be at Coach Wilson's street. I was starting to run out of gas. My legs were feeling like rubber. I struggled to keep my form. Coach told us that repeating a few words in our head could help us focus when we got tired. He called it a mantra. *I can make it. . . I can make it . . . I can make it,* I said over and over to myself.

Spruce Street — that was it! I knew that Tanner and Tania lived on this street too, but I had no clue which house was theirs. I blasted past three houses until I saw number 214 at the entrance to a brown bungalow. Coach's place. I ran up the driveway and leaped up the front stairs two at a time. My finger punched the doorbell like I was clicking the controller on my video game. *Ding . . . ding . . . ding . . . ding . . . ding!*

"Come on!" I shouted, rain streaking down my face. "Open the door! You've got to be home!"

But the door didn't budge. I stabbed the doorbell

again. Still no response. I looked in the front window to see if Coach was home. There was no sign of life. I took a deep breath and ran back down the stairs into the storm.

# 13 RESCUE 911

I felt like I was going to puke. Somehow I had run through the wind and the rain and the pain all the way back to the club. If it wasn't for the dry-land training, I never would have made it. Now I was rocking up and down on the dock as the waves crashed below. And I felt like I was going to be sick.

I had no choice but to suck it up. Tanner could be lost and freezing out in the storm — or worse. Something had to be done now.

I ran to the end of the dock and untied the thick yellow rope that held the powerboat in place. It was heavy, but I pulled it hand-over-hand through the choppy water until the boat was even with the dock. I hopped in the back, slipped on a full red life jacket, and held on to the sides as I inched my way to the front seat. I didn't know if I could start the old engine but I had seen Coach Wilson do it a hundred times before. I pushed the gear lever on the side to Forward and turned the key. Once. Twice. Three times. Still nothing.

"Come on!" I screamed into the wind. Finally, on my fourth try the engine sputtered to life. "Yeah!"

I grabbed the wheel and steered the boat away from the dock. The craft launched forward and I held on. For the next ten seconds I was flying over the waves, the engine roaring behind me. I'd be out in the middle of the lake searching for Tanner in no time! Then the motor started to snort, shudder, and hiccup. I turned around and saw the engine shaking on the back of the boat. Just as suddenly as the engine had sprung to life, it gave one final wheezing gasp and died.

The boat heaved up and down. The waves bashed against the side. I had to hang on or I'd be thrown overboard. I looked around. Panic washed over me. I was drifting toward the rocks on shore. Another few minutes and the boat would be a giant pile of wooden matchsticks. I thought about diving into the water and swimming back to the dock. I just didn't know if I could make it against the waves. I was trapped.

"Cody!" The voice was faint, but I was sure I heard it. I turned to face the dock and there he was — Coach Wilson waving his arms. I watched as he lowered a K-1 into the choppy water and slid into the cockpit. He pointed the boat toward me and started paddling with short, powerful strokes. Even though the waves were battering the sides of his kayak, Coach was so strong he was able to cut a path straight to the drifting powerboat. A minute later he was beside me.

"Jump in the water and grab onto the back of the kayak!" Coach yelled. "I'll tow you back to shore."

I had to tell him about Tanner. "But what about . . ."

"Just do it! We can talk after we get to the dock," Coach shouted over the screaming wind.

I tightened my life jacket then jumped in and hung on to the back of the kayak. Coach dug his paddle in the raging water and swiftly turned the kayak back to shore. He paddled with the same fierce determination and soon we were beside the dock. I let go and pulled myself out of the water and up on the platform.

I couldn't wait another second. "Tanner's still out on the lake!" I shouted.

Coach Wilson's eyes widened. "What? I thought it was just you out here."

"He must have taken his kayak out early this morning, before the storm. I was trying to save him. That's why I was in the powerboat."

Coach Wilson remained calm. "Forget the powerboat. We'll get it later. Right now Tanner needs to be rescued. We've got to hurry!"

I gulped and stared at Coach. "What do you mean, *we*?"

Coach Wilson looked up at the grey sky. "The weather is bad, but I've paddled in worse. The forecast was for a flash storm. It should blow over soon."

If Coach had a plan I still didn't know what it was.

"What are you going to do?" I asked.

"First, I'm going to call 911. But by the time the emergency squad gets here it may be too late. Ghost Lake is pretty far from the city. So we're going to get the K-2 to rescue Tanner."

*Why would he want the two-man boat?* I wondered.

"And you're coming with me, Cody."

"What do you need me for?"

"We'll need all the power we can get to cut through the waves, and you're a strong paddler," Coach said as we ran into the boathouse.

"But I lost the race to Tanner."

Coach Wilson looked me in the eye. "Breaking your blade was just bad luck. You paddled a great race. You're just as good as Tanner."

A shot of confidence surged through me. I didn't know that was what Coach thought.

"Besides, if you hadn't broken your paddle I wouldn't be here right now," Coach said reaching into the paddle cabinet and tossing me a shiny black blade. "I just stopped in to drop off this new one for you."

After Coach Wilson made the emergency call on his cell, we pulled the long K-2 out of its rack. We each grabbed one end of the kayak and heaved it up onto our shoulders. We carried the sleek white boat as fast as we could down the hill to the dock. Rain still slashed my face. I could hardly see.

Suddenly, a big gust of wind hit me from the side. The power of the blast knocked me over. I couldn't let the kayak fall to the ground. The hull was thin and could easily be punctured if it hit the road. I had to protect the boat at all costs. I held on with both hands as I crashed to the pavement.

"Are you okay, Cody?"

"I'm fine," I yelled.

But I wasn't. I looked down and saw both my knees were scraped. At first, I thought they were just small scratches and I wasn't hurt. Then blood came gushing out of the two wounds. A couple of cuts weren't going to stop me. I scrambled up from the ground and hoisted the kayak back onto my sore shoulder. I stumbled the rest of the way down to the water.

We lowered the kayak onto the dock beside the splashing waves. What if Tanner was thrown overboard in the storm? What if his kayak was capsized upside-down? What if he was too weak to hang on to the back of the boat like I did? How were we going to get him back to shore? Trying to lift him into our kayak would just tip us into the water. Then all three of us would be in trouble. We needed another way to rescue Tanner.

Coach already had it figured out. "We need the emergency life raft!" he shouted above the wind. "You get the raft while I get the kayak ready."

I knew Coach still had to stretch the rubber spray skirts over the cockpits to keep the rain and waves from pouring into the kayak.

The yellow raft was tied up at the other end of

the dock. The small rubber boat bounced wildly in the water. The dock bucked under me as I wobbled toward the raft. I felt like I was riding a bronco in the rodeo at the Calgary Stampede. The waves from the lake rolled under the grey platform and exploded beneath its surface. I stumbled to the raft, untied the rope, and pulled it through the water back to our kayak. Coach tied the raft to the back of our boat so we could tow it behind us.

Streams of blood ran down my shins as I lowered myself into our K-2. The boat heaved up and down with every crashing wave. Holding both sides tightly, I climbed into the second cockpit. Coach Wilson would take the front opening and steer. Once sitting down, I snapped the spray skirt around my waist to keep the water out. I turned around to check the raft was tightly tied and double-checked that my life jacket was buckled up. I knew I was going to need it.

Coach swiveled around in his cockpit. "You ready, Cody?"

"Ready, Coach," I said.

"Let's go find Tanner."

We pushed the long kayak away from the dock with our paddles and headed out into the teeth of the storm. Sheets of rain fell out of the sky. Frothy white waves rolled up and over the sides of our boat, splashing icy water on my arms and chest. I pulled down my cap to protect my eyes, but all I could see was a wall of water.

*Stroke . . . stroke . . . stroke.* I tried to match Coach's pace and made sure my paddle hit the water at the same time as his. We had to keep our blades together. It was the best way to cut through the whitecaps that were cresting on top of the waves. We struggled to move forward. The raft tugged behind us and bounced crazily into the air with each passing wave.

My muscles ached from battling against the waves. My body shivered from the spraying water and the swirling wind. I knew if I was cold, then Tanner would be freezing. And that was if his boat was still sitting upright on the water. What if his kayak had flipped over? He didn't have a spray skirt over his cockpit. Water would have rushed in and filled it within seconds. There was no way he could keep paddling. He would have to abandon ship, turn the kayak upside-down and hold on. Luckily, the kayak would float.

I knew Tanner was out there somewhere. I kept paddling as hard as I could and started to yell. "Taaaaannerrrr!" My shouts disappeared into the storm, sounding barely more than whispers. The blasting of the wind and the waves were drowning out my calls. "Taaaaannerrrr!" I tried again. There was no reply — just the howl of the wind.

Coach turned the front of the kayak to the east and started to paddle downwind. Now we were flying, skimming over the waves. We covered more distance with one stroke than we had with ten fighting against the wind. Maybe going faster and farther would increase our chances of finding Tanner.

As I stabbed the water with my paddle I wondered, *what if it were me lost in the icy waters of the lake? Would I be scared? Would I panic? Would I have the courage to hold on until help came?* I didn't know the answers. All I knew was that if there was one person I'd want to rescue me, it was Coach Wilson. He was the strongest kayaker I had ever seen, no matter whether or not he had made the Olympic team. I looked up and saw his blades slashing through the swirling deep, his muscled arms straining against the power of the storm.

A flash of yellow floating on the waves caught my eye. "Is that a lifebelt?" I screamed.

Coach pointed the bow of the kayak in a new direction. We dug in deep and paddled as fast as we could to the bright object bobbing in the water. As we neared the yellow target in front of us, my heart sank. It wasn't Tanner at all, but one of the yellow buoys the club used to mark the racecourse. At least now we knew our position on the lake. Maybe Tanner had been here practising on the same course he would be racing on this weekend.

Coach thrust his left paddle into the water and turned the kayak again.

"Let's try heading north!" he shouted.

The wind kicked up, sending the waves crashing over the bow of the boat. We made hard and quick strokes trying to cut through the choppy water.

I called out again. "Taaaaannerrrr!" Still there was no answer.

The clock was ticking. It was hard to tell how long we had paddled. We had to find Tanner fast. We looked desperately, shooting glances to the left and right.

Then I spotted him.

"There he is!" I screamed into the wind.

"I see him!" Coach yelled, pointing to a small speck of yellow bouncing like a cork on the wild waves.

We paddled with all our might and shouted as the kayak knifed through the frothy whitecaps.

"Hang on, Tanner!"

Seconds later we were by his side.

"You're going to be okay!" I shouted.

Tanner was clinging to his capsized kayak. His bright yellow lifebelt kept him afloat and was holding his head out of the water. His eyes were filled with fear. The blood had drained out of his face. His cheeks were white and his lips were blue. He was shivering and I knew that soon he would start suffering from hypothermia. We had to get him to shore.

The waves rocked the kayak as we paddled to get the life raft right next to Tanner. "You've got to climb into the raft!" I screamed.

Tanner nodded his head. He grabbed the side of the slippery raft and tried to pull himself up. He was too weak.

"You've got to try!" I yelled.

Tanner pulled again and was able to get both arms over the edge.

"One more time!" I shouted.

Tanner reached across the raft for a handle and pulled with his last ounce of strength. His face grimaced as his body slowly inched its way up and over the round edge of the raft. He flopped in like a seal.

"Good work, Cody!" Coach Wilson shouted.

I turned to face Tanner lying in the raft. "Let's get you back to shore!"

Tanner blinked that he understood.

# 14 LIKE FATHER, LIKE SON

A few more strokes through the rolling waves and our kayak was floating next to the dock. I unbuttoned my cockpit cover and slid out, hoisting myself up onto the wet dock. I scrambled to my feet and grabbed the rope. I pulled the life raft toward the dock. Tanner lay motionless in the yellow craft. I knelt down on my bloodied knees and reached out to pull him onto the rocking surface.

"Give me your hand!" I screamed.

Tanner raised his right hand and I grabbed it, dragging his tired and stiff body across the life raft and onto the dock. Coach Wilson pulled the kayak onto the dock and tied the life raft back to the post.

I knelt beside Tanner. "Put your arm over my shoulder. We're going to get you inside."

I braced my legs and slowly helped him stand up. Coach positioned himself on his other side. With Tanner's full weight crumpled against our arms, we staggered up the path. The wind still whipped the pelting rain against our tired bodies as we stumbled toward shelter. We limped under the cover of the boathouse and lay Tanner down on a stack of dry towels. He was too weak to sit. It felt good to be out of the wind and the rain.

"We need something to keep him warm," Coach said.

I could hear the wail of sirens in the distance. I raced into the storage room and grabbed two padded blankets that were used to protect the kayaks. I wrapped the blankets around Tanner to start raising his body temperature.

"You're safe now," I said to Tanner, as he closed his eyes. A few seconds later a red-and-white ambulance pulled to a stop outside the boathouse doorway. Two emergency paramedics dressed in blue uniforms sprinted toward us. One carried a black box of emergency medical supplies.

"How long was he in the water?" one of the paramedics asked as she knelt beside Tanner.

"I don't know," I replied. "He was missing for over an hour, I guess," I said, trying to remember. It was all a blur in my mind. The time seemed to go so fast.

"He's lucky you found him when you did," she said, holding Tanner's wrist to check his pulse.

"He's going to be okay, right?" I asked.

"He looks stable, but we need to run some tests." She put a tight grey wrap around Tanner's arm to take his blood pressure. "Any longer in that cold lake and he could have been in grave danger."

The paramedic looked up at Coach Wilson. "You're a hero."

"I'm not the hero," Coach said. "The real hero is Cody. He was the one who discovered Tanner was out in the storm. He was the one who ran to try and find me. And he was the one who spotted Tanner floating out in the lake. Cody deserves all the credit. All I did was call 911."

"Yours was the second emergency call we'd received that someone was stranded out on the lake," the paramedic with the moustache said. Then, turning to me, he added, "You did a brave thing, son."

"I didn't think I was so brave. I mean, at first I didn't do anything. Then I just did what any other kid at the club would have done."

"Those are nasty cuts you have there," said the woman paramedic, spotting the blood trickling down my leg. "We've been so busy with your friend that we didn't notice you're hurt as well. You better sit down so I can bandage them up."

I knew my legs were scraped pretty bad, but I hadn't thought about them until now. All I could think about before was saving Tanner. But who did the second call to 911 come from? Had someone else seen us out on the lake? No one else was here from the club now.

After my knees were covered with big white pads,

I stood back and watched the paramedics continue to care for Tanner. Still wrapped in blankets, he was sipping from a cup of hot chocolate to warm him up on the inside. The treatment seemed to be working. He was still pale, but he was now able to sit up.

A parade of cars came screeching into the parking lot — a white police car followed by an expensive black Mercedes. I could understand why the police were here, but I had no idea who was driving the luxury sedan. The two front doors swung open and a man and woman stepped out, both wearing business suits. They slammed their doors shut and marched toward us. Their strides were long and their heels clicked with every step.

"Goodness me, Tanner," the woman said. "I'm glad you're okay, but what were you thinking?"

"I hope this teaches you a lesson," the man said.

"You could have drowned!" the woman said, staring down at Tanner. "We've just had to leave a meeting with some important clients to come get you. Your sister said you'd left for the club early this morning, but she hadn't heard from you since and was worried."

"Then we had to cancel another important meeting with the bankers in Calgary about the development, just to drive all the way out here to the lake," the man said, pointing his finger. "We've had to change a lot of plans just because of you."

Tanner looked up at the man and woman from

where he sat on the ground. "Sorry," he mumbled.

*These* were Tanner's parents? He had just spent the most frightening hour of his life clinging to a kayak in freezing waters. I couldn't believe what I was hearing. I know my parents wouldn't have acted this way. All they would have cared about is that I was safe. My mom would probably have been squeezing me like an orange by now.

It all started to make sense. Listening to how harsh Tanner's parents were made me realize why Tanner was the way he was. Why he didn't care about anyone else. Why he only looked out for himself. Tanner wasn't mean. He was just acting like his mom and dad.

The paramedic stood up from Tanner's side. "This might be a good time to check whether your son is okay, Ma'am," he said.

"I guess you're right," Tanner's mom said, looking around and seeing everyone staring at her. "When can we take him home?" She bent over and lightly touched Tanner's shoulder.

"I'm afraid you can't," the paramedic said. "He's been through a lot. I think it's best if we take him to the hospital for observation. Let the doctors have a look at him to make sure there are no lasting effects from the hypothermia."

"Well, if you really think that's necessary," his dad said.

The two paramedics eased Tanner onto a stretcher

and gently carried him toward the waiting ambulance. I stood watching as Mr. and Mrs. Blake walked alongside their son, still scolding him for ruining their day. I thought Tanner might wave goodbye or say something to me, but I didn't really expect it. It was Tanner after all. *Some people never change,* I thought to myself.

"Wait a minute," Tanner said to the paramedics. The stretcher stopped and he looked at me between his parents. "Hey, Cody," he said, weakly reaching out his hand in a clenched ball. "Thanks man — you saved my life."

We bumped fists. And then he was gone.

# 15 THE BEST MEDICINE

Coach and I walked down the long sterile hallway of the hospital. It had been several hours since the danger on the lake. The storm had cleared up and it turned into a nice, sunny day. I'd accepted Coach's offer of a ride into town to visit Tanner. I'd spent the last few hours trying to make sense of everything that had happened. Sure, Tanner had come on strong when he arrived, but I hadn't been very welcoming to him either.

As we approached Tanner's room, I noticed Tania was sitting on a chair in the hall. I still hadn't said anything to her since I'd found out she was Tanner's sister.

"Coach, you go in. I'll just be a minute."

"Sure, Cody."

I sat down in an empty chair beside Tania, but she didn't turn to look at me.

"Look, Tania. I'm sorry I didn't call you. It's just that —"

"You know what, Cody? You might think Tanner's a jerk, and that he has a big ego, but you're just the same as him. And at least he can be nice. When our parents are never home, who do you think takes care of me? Tanner. He's not who you think he is."

"I know. I'm sorry. I just couldn't believe it when I found out you were his sister. I mean, you're so nice and friendly. You seem like opposites. And Tanner hated me, too, don't forget. I knew it wouldn't be long until he turned you against me. I already thought he had turned Logan and Coach against me."

"I'm this way because Tanner gives me all the attention that my parents are too busy to give us. He's my big brother and he has a big heart, Cody. The tough-guy thing is nothing but an act. You should give him a chance."

"I guess you're right. Kayaking was the first thing I was ever good at. And when Tanner got here and he was better than me, well, I guess I didn't really welcome him to the team like I should have."

"You know I'm right," Tania said, turning her brown eyes on me. "When I saw you down the street banging on Coach's door in the storm I knew something was really wrong. That's when I called 911."

She smiled and leaned over to give me a hug. "Thanks, Cody. You saved us."

★ ★ ★

When Coach left Tanner's room to get coffee, I went in.

Tanner was lying in the hospital bed. He looked white as a ghost. His eyes were thin slits and fluttered as he struggled to open them. He raised a single finger and pointed for me to come nearer. I took a few steps from the doorway and sat down beside his bed.

His voice was barely a whisper. "Is that you, Cody?"

"I'm right here, Tanner," I said softly.

"Bring your face a little closer so I can see it one last time," he croaked.

Was this it? Were these going to be Tanner's last words? Were the ice-cold waters of the lake too much for him? Did we take too long to come to the rescue? I leaned in as close as I dared to hear him better.

Suddenly, Tanner sprang up like a jack-in-a-box. His eyes popped open and his mouth let out a wild cry, "Gotcha!" Then he burst out laughing.

At first I thought he must be delirious. That it must be some crazy reaction to the hypothermia. But as Tanner continued to laugh I realized he had totally fooled me.

I started to laugh, too, partly from being sucked in by the joke and partly from the relief of knowing Tanner was going to be okay.

Once we started laughing together we couldn't stop. We just fed off each other. Before yesterday I never thought I'd see the day when Tanner and I would be able to stand being in the same room with each other, let alone sharing a joke. But rescuing him had changed all that. Now I knew him better. I've seen him with his busy lawyer parents. I knew what he'd had to deal with. I get what makes him tick. He's not so bad. We actually have stuff in common. Like going fast in a kayak, and trying to prank the other guy when he least expects it.

"What's so funny?" Coach said, walking in carrying a hot coffee from the vending machine down the hall.

"Nothing," Tanner said.

"Yeah, nothing," I said.

"Well, I'm glad you're feeling better, Tanner," Coach said. "You had us pretty worried."

"I know," Tanner said, shaking his head. "Even though I didn't know bad weather was coming, I was a doofus for going out on the water by myself."

"I tried to phone both you guys and warn you about the storm," Coach said.

"I was just trying to get in one more training session," Tanner replied.

"I know how important the nationals are to you," Coach Wilson nodded. "But there will be other races. You've got to get healthy now. After today, neither one of you is fit for the K-1. That event is too hard unless you're in top shape and well rested. The rescue knocked a lot out of both of you."

I was a little disappointed. I thought maybe I would take Tanner's place in the K-1. But Coach was right. Even now I felt my body starting to crash and my eyes get heavy.

"I think I'll enter Nick in the singles race," Coach Wilson said. "He finished third behind you guys in our club race."

"What about the K-2?" I asked.

Coach Wilson looked at me. "Let's see how you're feeling in a few days, Cody. If you've got your energy back, maybe you and Logan can team up."

"What about me?" Tanner asked, looking hopeful from his bed. "I'm feeling good as new." Even though Tanner said he was perfectly fine, he still looked a little grey.

"Let's see what the doc says," Coach said.

# 16 BEHIND DOOR NUMBER ONE

The morning of the nationals, I sat eating a big bowl of cereal and listening to the weather forecast on the radio. This time the voice was upbeat. "Blue skies are forecast all weekend long for the Calgary area," the broadcaster said. *That's more like it,* I thought.

My arm muscles weren't sore anymore and the cuts on my knees had started to heal. I'd replaced the big white bandages with smaller ones. The scabs were gross and cool at the same time. I may not have been one-hundred percent, but I was getting close.

Mom and Dad came into the kitchen together. I was surprised to see that they were smiling again this week, after so many serious conversations about the café being sold and torn down. I'd spent most of the past few days at home, recovering. Tania had even come over one night to watch TV with us.

"How're you feeling today, Cody?" Mom asked.

My mouth full of cereal, I nodded that I was fine.

"Ready for race day, champ?" Dad asked.

"Before you go," Mom said, "there's something important your dad and I need to talk to you about."

I put down my spoon and waited.

"The day of the storm," Mom began, "your dad and I left early in the morning for an appointment in Calgary. We met the developers of the golf course there and their lawyers — the Blakes. We made a case for preserving and protecting the lake and the surrounding area. It took a bit of convincing, but we think we've got the developers to agree to help fund a nature reserve. It will be a lot of work, but your dad and I have agreed to manage an environmental learning centre on the reserve — no one knows the area around here better than he does."

"Wow! That's awesome!"

My parents grinned at me. "We were pretty upset when your mom found out she was going to lose her job. Then we realized that even though we couldn't stop what was happening, we could still work together to put a positive spin on the outcome," Dad said.

I thought then about what happened between Tanner and me when he got here. Instead of trying to work with Tanner and build a better team, I'd driven a wedge between us. And now to find out that his parents had been involved in the changes that had been happening to the land around the Blue Water! I started to laugh. I guess we could all learn a lesson or two about how to deal with change.

# Behind Door Number One

★ ★ ★

I arrived early at the club to get ready for the regatta. Even though I hoped Coach would pick me to race later, I still wanted to volunteer. He said I could help give the paddlers their lane numbers for each event. Plus, I wanted to cheer on the other members of our club who would be competing. We had a bunch of ace athletes in the older midget and junior categories who would be in the hunt for gold, silver, and bronze. It's not every day you get a chance to watch your team go head-to-head against the best kayakers in the country.

There was a newspaper article pinned to the bulletin board in the lounge of the club that told of the rescue. The picture above it showed Tanner in his hospital bed, flanked by Coach on one side, and me and Tania on the other. It was hard to believe the storm was only a couple of days ago. It felt like a week.

Coach seemed more easygoing with all the guys now. Almost as if the rescue had gotten rid of all his bad memories. He didn't seem so disappointed over losing out at a chance at the Olympic team. Saving someone's life means a lot more than any race.

The parking lot was jam-packed. By nine o'clock in the morning the club was crawling with hundreds of athletes and spectators. Everywhere I looked, groups of people were forming circles all over the grounds. Each circle was a team from a different province with a different colour. The kayakers from Ontario were wearing their red racing singlets. Nova Scotia was in black, Quebec in white, Saskatchewan in green. Our team from Alberta was dressed in blue, just like the provincial flag that flew over the boathouse. There were so many athletes and giant coloured circles splashed together in one place it was like watching a mini-Olympics with its five-ring symbol. All that was missing was a giant flame.

All my friends had volunteered for different jobs. I scanned the beehive of activity and saw Nick and Nate working at the concession stand offering power bars and other snacks to hungry paddlers and spectators. I searched a bit further and spied Kai and Tania selling souvenir T-shirts. Each shirt had a pair of crossed paddles on the front with the words "*Canadian Kayak Championships*" printed above them. I had been stashing cash from my allowance to buy one.

Far off I spotted a tall skinny kid snaking through the clusters of people searching for someone. I looked again and saw a tuft of frizzy red hair. It was Logan! I bet he was searching for me. I raced down the stairs and darted through the crowd to meet him. He didn't give me a chance to speak.

"Whoa, dude! I've been looking all over for you. Coach wants to see you."

"I bet he wants to know if I'm ready for the K-2 race," I guessed.

"I don't know, but it sounded important," Logan

said, out of breath. "He said to meet him in the coaches' office right away."

The office was deep inside the boathouse, past all the kayak racks and down a long, dimly lit hall. The room was crammed with four old oak desks and the walls were plastered with big posters of Adam van Koeverden, showing his gold-medal paddling technique. I walked down the corridor, wondering who Coach would pair me with for the K-2 event. I figured it would be Kai, since that's who he mentioned the other night. We would be an okay team, but we wouldn't rock like Tanner and I would if he wasn't recovering in the hospital.

I knocked on the closed door. "Come on in, Cody," Coach Wilson said. "We were expecting you."

I swung the door open and my jaw dropped. Sitting right next to the coach was Tanner — and he was wearing his blue racing singlet!

"I thought you might be surprised to see me," Tanner laughed.

"I am, man, but this is the kind of surprise I like."

"I was just talking with Tanner," Coach said, leaning forward in his chair. "The doctor has given him a clean bill of health. He's feeling a lot better since the storm, but he still doesn't think he has the energy to race by himself in the K-1."

"I know what he means," I said nodding. "I'm still getting my strength back as well."

"So here's my question," Coach said looking back and forth between us. "Do you guys have enough in the tank to compete in the K-2?"

Tanner smiled and looked me square in the eyes. "You're an awesome paddler, Cody, and you showed a lot of guts saving me. I know you'd never give up in a race. I'd be totally stoked being your partner."

I didn't have to think for more than a split second. This wasn't just a chance to race in a K-2. This was a chance to race for gold in the Canadian Nationals.

"I'm with you, partner," I said, slapping Tanner five.

Tanner and I were just about to walk out the door when Coach Wilson stopped me.

"One more thing, Cody," he said, tossing me a Team Alberta blue singlet. "This is for you."

# 17 SILVER LINING

"Would Tanner Blake and Cody Flynn please whip-in for the K-2 race?" The announcement boomed from the big black speakers that hung high above the crowd. It was go time.

"Let's get our kayak," I said to Tanner.

"Follow me," he said, leading the way into the boathouse.

We pulled out a white K-2, lifted the boat onto our shoulders, and headed to the official's table to get our race numbers.

"You boys from Alberta?" the race official asked, standing at the whip-in table.

Tanner and I answered at the same time. "Yes, sir."

"You're a little late. We didn't know if you were racing or not."

I looked at Tanner and grinned. "Neither did we."

"Team Alberta is in lane three," the official said loudly, handing us sticky white squares of paper with the number three on them. "You better hustle."

We quickly stuck one number to our shirts and one to the main deck of the kayak. There wasn't a second to waste.

Coach Wilson scrambled beside us as we rushed the kayak down to the water.

"Remember, the K-2 is a team competition," he said. "You have to work together."

"But we've never paddled together before," I said, concentrating on carrying the back of the kayak. My bandaged knees were still shaky and I didn't want to crash to the ground like I did in the storm.

"Three days ago you paddled the K-2 with me through whitecaps," Coach Wilson said. "You were strong and determined. If you can do that, you can do anything."

Coach's words gave me a shot of confidence, but still I was unsure. Paddling with a super-strong coach who should have been in the Olympics is one thing. Paddling with a guy fresh out of hospital in a boat you've never shared before is a whole other ball game.

Tanner and I lowered our kayak into the water beside the dock. I rested my paddle across the rear cockpit for support and climbed in.

The race hadn't started and we were already behind. The boats from the other four provinces were paddling way ahead of us toward the starting line out in the middle of the lake. The race would begin in only a couple of minutes. We had to fly.

Tanner swiveled around in his cockpit and stuck out his fist. "Ready, partner?"

I knocked it hard then flipped around my hat. "Let's do this."

We pushed off from the dock and paddled toward the biggest challenge of our racing lives. Our blades slashed through the glassy surface as we tried to catch the other teams. With the power of two paddlers we knifed through the water. I knew we were wasting too much energy, but we had no choice. We couldn't be late for the start.

A minute later we pulled alongside the other teams. Red, green, blue, black, and white boats from five provinces were spread out evenly across the starting line. Each kayak was pointed between the bright yellow lane markers. Each athlete sat tight as a spring, waiting to uncoil his power. Only the gentle ripples of the lake broke the silence.

The boats from Ontario and Nova Scotia floated in the outside lanes, one and five. Saskatchewan and British Columbia bobbed up and down in lanes two and four. That left Tanner and me in lane three, smack-dab in the middle.

*Brrraaarrr!* The horn from the judge's boat blared to signal the start. This was it. The race was on. I put my head down and punched my paddle into the water on the right side of the kayak. We launched forward, but our takeoff was jerky. Our thin boat rocked from side to side. I looked up and saw why. Tanner had started to paddle on the left — the opposite side from me! We were out of sync right from the first stroke, and it was my fault.

I should have known better. Tanner was the "stroke" in our boat — the paddler in front who decides which side to stroke on and how fast. He can't turn around to see what I'm doing. I have to follow him. All the teams from the other provinces knew this. They had practised together for weeks, months, maybe years. They knew both the front and back paddlers had to stroke at the same time on the same side. You had to paddle together to maximize your speed and power. The other boats shot ahead.

I made a quick adjustment. I followed Tanner's lead and copied him stroke for stroke. When his left blade hit the water, my left blade hit the water. All of a sudden we were skimming across the sparkling blue surface of the lake. Our paddles flashed through the water in perfect unison. We were twins flying down the racecourse. I couldn't see the two outside lanes but we were gaining on Saskatchewan and British Columbia in the middle.

*Pull . . . pull . . . pull.* I focused all my attention on making clean strokes. I could almost hear Coach in my head. *"Wait until your blade is fully submerged before dragging it through the water. If you see splashing, you're just wasting your effort."* I looked down. There wasn't a splash in sight. There was no stopping us.

By the halfway point of the 1,000-metre race our hard work was paying off. Tanner and I had drawn even with the other four teams. I could see them out of the corner of my eye. All five boats were slashing through the water in a straight line. It was anybody's race to win.

A few seconds later I wasn't so sure. I looked over my shoulder and couldn't believe what I saw. The teams on either side of us were pulling away. Both Saskatchewan and British Columbia had put their pace into overdrive. They must have been hitting eighty strokes a minute!

I didn't know how Tanner was feeling. Did he have any juice left to respond to the challenge? All the cards were stacked against us. We were both tired from the storm. Tanner had spent an hour in freezing waters. I had spent an hour running and fighting angry waves to rescue him. We didn't know we were going to race until just minutes before the start. We had paddled in a fury to make it on time. *Did we have anything left?*

I looked straight ahead and got my answer. Tanner was digging in harder than I had ever seen him. His paddle flashed from side to side. His blades churned through the water. He was matching the pace of the other teams stroke for stroke. Watching his supercharged effort gave me a shot of adrenaline. I didn't know how long I could keep it up, but I was going to give it everything I had.

We bolted ahead. Saskatchewan, British Columbia, and Nova Scotia couldn't maintain the wicked pace.

Their three boats were falling behind. Only two boats were left to battle it out. It was just the red of Ontario against our blue of Alberta. We battled on.

It was a scorching day. The sun burned down on us. Small drops of sweat exploded on my forehead and ran into my eyes. I blinked hard to clear them. My arms were slick with a mix of sweat and spray flying off my paddle. Every muscle in my body hurt. Every beat of my heart pounded. I thought my lungs were going to burst. Just one more minute to go.

"Come on, Tanner!" I shouted.

There they were. The big red buoys of the finish line lay dead ahead. *Stroke . . . stroke . . . stroke.* Tanner and I put our heads down and buried our blades in the deep blue water. I couldn't see the boat from Ontario. Were they even? Were they ahead? I didn't look. Even though my arms were numb with pain I kept my form. I wasn't going to let our team down with another mistake like that. Ten seconds. Five seconds. I plunged my paddle into the water one last time. Then it was over. We had crossed the finish line.

I didn't know who had won. I was too tired and too afraid to look. I slumped forward gasping for breath. I could see Tanner collapse in front of me. He lay lifeless against the front edge of the cockpit. He had given every ounce of effort not just for himself, but for the team. You could question Tanner's bad attitude of the past, but you could never question his effort today. He had sacrificed everything for this race. Slowly, Tanner sat up and leaned back. Without turning he reached out his hand toward me.

"We did it, partner."

The three trailing boats raced across the finish line. The splashing of their blades stopped as if taking even one more stroke was impossible. Lungs gulped in oxygen. Silence hung in the air.

We drifted across the ripples of the lake. Finally, I had the courage to look over at lane one. Two boys in red shirts were lifting their paddles high over their heads. Team Ontario had won.

Coach Wilson would tell us later that the race was a dead heat until the very end. He said the two paddlers from Ontario had leaned way back and shot their kayak across the finish line with their last stroke. They had won by the tip of a boat — a single tick of the stopwatch.

Somehow it didn't matter. Half an hour ago I didn't have a partner or the chance to race in a national championship. Now I had a new friend and a silver medal to hang around my neck. Coach Wilson said he had never been more proud. That he had never seen an effort filled with more bravery and heart — not even at the Olympics.

Tanner and I sat up straight. We pointed our boat toward the shore and paddled home.

# BE A
# PRO! KNOW THE LINGO.

Part of being a successful kayaker is not only knowing when it's safe to be on the water, but also being familiar with some important kayaking terms. Here are the definitions of the kayaking terms used in this book.

**BOATHOUSE:** The building where all the kayaks and paddles are stored.

**COCKPIT:** The opening of the kayak where you sit and paddle.

**DUMP:** Sprint racing kayaks are very narrow and can tip, or dump, into the water if you're not careful.

**K-1, K-2, K-4:** Sprint kayaks come in three lengths for one, two, and four paddlers.

**REGATTA:** A big competition where paddlers from different clubs race.

**SINGLET:** A special team shirt without sleeves used for races.

**SPRAY SKIRT:** A rubber cover that snaps over the cockpit of a kayak to keep out the water.

**WHIP-IN:** The process of checking-in with a regatta official to get your lane number before a race.

# OTHER BOOKS YOU'LL ENJOY IN THE SPORTS STORIES SERIES

## BASKETBALL

❏ *Fast Break* by Michael Coldwell

Moving from Toronto to small-town Nova Scotia was rough, but when Jeff makes the school basketball team he thinks things are looking up.

❏ *Camp All-Star* by Michael Coldwell

In this insider's view of a basketball camp, Jeff Lang encounters some unexpected challenges.

❏ *Nothing but Net* by Michael Coldwell

The Cape Breton Grizzly Bears prepare for an out-of-town basketball tournament they're sure to lose.

❏ *Slam Dunk* by Steven Barwin and Gabriel David Tick

In this sequel to *Roller Hockey Blues*, Mason Ashbury's basketball team adjusts to the arrival of some new players: girls.

❏ *Courage on the Line* by Cynthia Bates

After Amelie changes schools, she must confront difficult former teammates in an extramural match.

❏ *Free Throw* by Jacqueline Guest

Matthew Eagletail must adjust to a new school, a new team and a new father along with five pesky sisters.

❏ *Triple Threat* by Jacqueline Guest

Matthew's cyber-pal Free Throw comes to visit, and together they face a bully on the court.

❏ *Queen of the Court* by Michele Martin Bossley

What happens when the school's fashion queen winds up on the basketball court?

# ICE HOCKEY

❏ *Deflection!* by Bill Swan

Jake and his two best friends play road hockey together and are members of the same league team. But some personal rivalries and interference from Jake's three all-too-supportive grandfathers start to create tension among the players.

❏ *Misconduct* by Beverly Scudamore

Matthew has always been a popular student and hockey player. But after an altercation with a tough kid named Dillon at hockey camp, Matt finds himself number one on the bully's hit list.

❏ *Roughing* by Lorna Schultz Nicholson

Josh is off to an elite hockey camp for the summer, where his roommate, Peter, is skilled enough to give Kevin, the star junior player, some serious competition, creating trouble on and off the ice.

❏ *Home Ice* by Beatrice Vandervelde

Leigh Aberdeen is determined to win the hockey championship with a new, all girls team, the Chinooks.

❏ *Against the Boards* by Lorna Schultz Nicholson

Peter has made it onto an AAA Bantam team and is now playing hockey in Edmonton. But this shy boy from the Northwest Territories is having a hard time adjusting to his new life.

❏ *Delaying the Game* by Lorna Schultz Nicholson

When Shane comes along, Kaleigh finds herself unsure whether she can balance hockey, her friendships, and this new dating-life.

❏ *Two on One* by C.A. Forsyth

When Jeff's hockey team gets a new coach, his sister Melody starts to get more attention as the team's shining talent.

❏ *Icebreaker* by Steven Barwin

Gregg Stokes can tell you exactly when his life took a turn for the worse. It was the day his new stepsister, Amy, joined the starting line-up of his hockey team.

# SOCCER